T0290363

PENGUIN BOOKS

STEADY SARAH

Justine Camacho-Tajonera was born and raised in Cebu City, Philippines. Despite starting a corporate career in telecommunications, she pursued her master's degree in Literature and Cultural Studies to keep her close to her first love of writing (and reading). She has had her poetry published in several anthologies and local publications, and has self-published several books in various genres. She maintains a personal blog, *Claiming Alexandria*. She is a marketing professional in the Philippines, is married, and has two children.

STEADY
SARAH

JUSTINE CAMACHO-TAJONERA

PENGUIN BOOKS
An imprint of Penguin Random House

PENGUIN BOOKS

Penguin Books is an imprint of the Penguin Random House group of
companies whose addresses can be found at
global.penguinrandomhouse.com

Published by Penguin Random House SEA Pte Ltd
40 Penjuru Lane, #03-12, Block 2
Singapore 609216

First published in Penguin Books by Penguin Random House SEA 2024

ISBN 9789815204728

Typeset in Garamond by MAP Systems, Bengaluru, India

www.penguin.sg

For V

Act 1

The Road

CHAPTER 1

I wish I were elsewhere, Sarah briefly thought while she boarded the taxi she had commissioned through an app at six in the morning. She quickly brushed away the thought, grateful that she could afford a safe taxi and that she was on her way to see her boyfriend, Pete. She actually would have wanted to head home first because she had a tough night at TechConnect, the business process outsourcing firm she worked for, but Pete said that it was important. She tried to keep her eyes open, but she was just too tired. She loved her job, but, sometimes, she just wanted a break. Her car passed a Department of Tourism billboard showcasing a local destination: a lone kayaker paddling through an expanse of blue ocean, heading towards the beach. *What about there?*

She fished around in her handbag for her phone trying to think of the last to-do that had been swimming in her head. She remembered that she wanted to email Richard, her client rep, about his next visit. He had missed his last trip, and all her reports were going through conference call or email, which she hated because a lot of stuff she wanted to communicate just didn't get through. She mentally composed an email, but the fatigue got to her before she could even take out her phone to type a draft.

The driver woke her up at half past six because she had reached her destination. For Sarah, it seemed like she had just closed her eyes for a few seconds. The sun was shining brightly already. She put on her shades and walked into the 24/7 café and looked for a dark corner where she could get a few minutes of peace before Pete arrived.

'Sorry for being late,' Pete said. It was only a few minutes, really, but Pete was like that, a stickler for punctuality. Sarah looked up and smiled. He was already dressed for work in a crisp polo, looking handsome as usual but a little worse for wear with a hint of dark circles under his eyes. That usually happened to him when he clocked in overtime at the treasury department of Pilipinas Bank & Trust Co. 'Can I get you coffee?'

'No, no thanks, Pete. I want to sleep as soon as I get home. Maybe some chamomile tea, instead.'

'Breakfast?'

'You know my usual.'

'Okay.'

That was the nice thing about their relationship. They knew everything there was to know about each other. Sarah did not have to get confused over what Pete liked (favourite colour: dark blue; music: classical, jazz, or none at all; favourite time of day: morning; favourite food: olive oil pasta or Ilocos longganisa from his mom's hometown with garlic fried rice; favourite beverage: black coffee).

Pete came back with a tray: her favourite toast and omelette with chamomile tea and just black coffee for him.

'So, why couldn't this wait again?' Sarah asked Pete before she took a sip of chamomile. For some reason, she felt butterflies in her stomach. Not the pleasant kind.

'Why don't you get something to eat first?' he said.

Uh-oh. That was definitely a sign that there was something wrong. She forced herself to eat the omelette even though she couldn't really taste it any more, and the butter made her queasy.

'What is it, Pete?' Sarah asked again when she was done with her toast. She couldn't stand the suspense. He looked unusually pale as he watched her finish her breakfast. She didn't want to imagine what he was going to say. *Is he going to break up with me?* The thought came unbidden, but it came from her gut.

'Sarah, I don't know where to start but I just wanted to talk to you already because something's been bothering me the past couple of days.'

Sarah frowned. If something had been bothering him, he would have called earlier, not a couple of days later.

'We've been together since college. I think it's time for us to see other people.' *Boom.* There it was.

'Is there someone else, Pete?' Sarah suspected there was someone else because this kind of thing wouldn't be urgent if there wasn't anyone else in the picture.

'It's not what you think.' Right. There *was* someone else. She could read him so well.

'I think we've been growing apart since you got promoted,' Pete added.

'Pete, just answer the question.'

'There is someone else but it's not the main reason why I want us to end our relationship.'

'Of course it is. You don't need to bullshit with me, okay?'

'We haven't been seeing each other much. You're just too exhausted from work to be in a relationship.' Actually, that was true and it hurt. A lot.

'And so you go have a fling?' Sarah felt her face grow hot. She didn't raise her voice, but she felt tears coming on.

'It's not a fling. I want to come clean with you and move on.'

'How long have you been seeing her?'

'Joanna and I are not dating, okay? We worked on a project together. That's all. But this isn't about her.'

'Finally, a name. No, this isn't about her, Pete. This is about you.'

'No, this is about us.'

'Apparently, there is no "us" any more, right?' This time, Sarah couldn't stop the tears from falling. Six years went down the drain.

I wish I were elsewhere. There was that thought again. But she didn't have the luxury of granted wishes. She closed her eyes, took a deep breath, and mentally counted to ten.

'Okay, Pete, here's what we'll do. Let's split the joint account we had based on contribution. As I remember it, it's 60/40 in my favour. Let's give it a week. You're the one working in the bank, so you take care of all the paperwork. I'll give you the account where you can deposit my share.' It was a good thing they didn't leave stuff with each other like books, shirts, or whatnot. 'There will be no return of gifts. Gifts are gifts. They're considered given.' Sarah wanted to press 'pause'. In her fatigued state, she just wanted to curl up in her bed and not have to deal with what was going on. She forced herself to go numb so she could deal with Pete.

'This isn't just about money, Sarah. Why are we going straight to that?'

'I know. But I'm not going to go through a "let's give this one more try" routine. When you say it's over then it's over. All there is to do is sort out the joint account.'

'I was just trying to explain to you why this even happened.'

'So you can blame me?'

'No, I didn't say that.' He didn't need to. Didn't he just imply that she neglected him because of her promotion?

'Look, Pete. You said it yourself. You want to come clean with me. So let's just make this a clean break, okay?'

'I thought we'd need more time.'

What kind of wimp do you think I am? 'Pete, I don't need more time. I just want this to be over as soon as possible.' *And I don't want to spend another minute with a cheater like you in my sight.*

'I've been feeling lonely in our relationship. Doesn't that count in this conversation?'

Sarah felt a twinge of guilt. However, she didn't feel the need to prolong the agony. She could feel the weight of their six years together on her shoulders.

'Pete, if you wanted us to work on our relationship, I would have given this more time. But you clearly want to see someone else, right? You go on and do that. The rest is just a waste of time.'

'This isn't completely my fault.'

'Does this even matter any more?'

'It does to me.'

Sarah didn't have a ring on her finger. She wished she did just so she could fling it at him. She remembered the day they decided on a joint account. On a whim, their date had turned into a condo-hunting adventure. One particular condo caught her eye. It had a modern glass façade, but the interiors were more Zen and Scandinavian, with smooth bleached wood accents and lots of natural light streaming into the hallways. 'You like it,' Pete had observed. 'I can see us living here,' Sarah had confessed to him. He had held her hand. 'Then, let's save up for it.' It was that simple. She didn't need a fancy proposal.

'I thought we had a future together. I thought you would cut me some slack for the extra pressure at work. I thought wrong.'

'I'm sorry. It's just that I didn't feel like I was in a relationship any more.'

'Look, if you really cared, you would have given me more time to adjust. You wouldn't have skipped over this to the next available girl out there.'

'That is unfair.'

'You know what's unfair? What's unfair is the amount of time I invested in us.'

'Why is it always about calculations to you, Sarah? Okay, if it's calculations you want, I'll give you one. How many hours did you spend with me in the last month?'

Sarah knew the answer to the question, but she couldn't bring herself to say it.

'Look, Pete, I'm not interested in getting the last word. Or even being right. I just want to get some sleep. I don't think there's anything left for me to say.'

'I don't want to end this on a negative note.'

'Well, too late, Pete.'

She refused his offer to drive her home. She got herself another taxi and cried all the way home. That joint account was for their 'future'. They had plans. And now it was all gone. Sarah wasn't just grieving over the end of their relationship. She was also angry. How could she not have seen this coming? And why was Pete trying to pin the blame on her? She knew he wasn't entirely wrong. But here she was holding the shorter end of the stick while he moved on to some girl named Joanna.

CHAPTER 2

Sarah woke up late on Sunday. She had cried herself to sleep the night before. Between bouts of muffled weeping (she didn't want anyone to hear at home), she agonized over her social media relationship status and whether she should delete Pete's number from her phone. 'Single' was now on her 'About' page. She had deleted his phone number, but it was useless. She still remembered it. Remembering was something she was good at.

She remembered the first time she saw him during freshman orientation. He was wearing a crisp white polo shirt and jeans. He was also the cutest guy she'd seen so far, clean-cut look, square jaw, and puppy dog eyes. She wasn't sure about the building she was headed to, and she hadn't spotted her childhood friends in the crowd, so she took her chances and talked to the first good-looking boy on her radar. When he smiled at her, revealing the deep dimples on his cheeks, she was a goner.

Pete was always so gentle. He was always so patient. She just couldn't believe that he was out of her life. Just like that. Should she have begged him to stay? She played the conversation they had in the café over and over in her mind. What if she'd done things differently? What if she hadn't been so proud?

But it was too late. And she had her nth bout of ugly crying. Seeing her vision board on her desk didn't make things any better. The headline was 'Positive Change'. She had cut out and stuck on the left side of the board a woman in workout clothes showing off her abs. On the right side was a woman working on a laptop with fan-like arrangements of cash beside her. At the centre of the board was a beautiful bride in white lace beside a handsome groom in a suit. On the lower left side was a minimalist, brand new condo with soft grey furniture, blush-coloured pillows, and muted lighting coming from behind gauzy white curtains. On the lower right side was a picture of a couple in a tropical paradise.

Pete hadn't proposed. Yet. But she had always thought this year would be their year. That was why she had worked so hard for her promotion. They were supposed to make their condo down payment this year. The deadline was in a few months. And that was why she had always thought that this year would be the year they'd marry. This was not the change she had in mind. 'Now what?' she asked herself before dissolving into another bout of tears.

It was afternoon when Sarah heard a knock on her door.

'Are you okay, honey?' Sarah's mom asked.

'I'm okay!' She gathered all the used tissues on her bed and stashed them under a pillow. She knew that after her mom knocked, she'd open the door without asking if it was okay. Sure enough, her mom stepped in. She was dressed in a loose shirt and frayed denim jeans, a sign that she was doing chores or one of her mini-craft projects in the garage.

She took one look at Sarah's face and said, 'No, you're not.'

'I'll *be* okay,' Sarah insisted.

'Do you want to talk about it?'

'Not right now.'

'Would you at least have some lunch?'

'I'm just not hungry. I'll be down in a bit.'

Her mom pulled down her blanket and reached for her arm.

'Seriously, Ma, you know that I'll do what I say.'

Her mom threw her a hurt look.

'I promise,' Sarah said as she sat up.

'Okay, I'll see you at the dining table. Just let me know when you want to talk, just you and me.'

'I will.'

Before getting up, Sarah checked her phone. She had a message from Benito, one of her best friends: *How's Steady Sarah doing?* She texted back: *Steady Sarah is doing just fine.* Sarah smiled. She was glad that she had trusted friends like Benito who had her back. She went on to wash her face and get rid of her puffy nose and eyes with a little concealer.

As Sarah got dressed, she wondered if she ought to move out of her mom's house (technically, her dad's house) even though things didn't turn out as she'd planned with Pete. It was nice that her mom was always there for her. But sometimes it was cloying. The thing was, she knew that she couldn't just leave her mom. Her mom couldn't figure out the remote control of the TV or, worse, the Wi-Fi. What would her mom do without her? Frankly, Sarah felt that she was playing 'mom' to her own mom a lot of times. It just wouldn't work out if she had her own place. Ever since her dad left the family when she was only seven, she'd seen too much of her mom falling apart. She just couldn't risk it. And, of course, there was Miguel, her younger brother. He was still in high school. She just couldn't leave him with her mom. Sarah took a deep breath before stepping out of her room. That was who she was: Steady Sarah. Keeping it together was her job even when she felt hollow inside.

'What are your plans today?' her mom asked.

Sarah could see that look on her face, the one that seemed nonchalant but was lined with deep worry. Sarah made sure that her mom saw her put a spoonful of rice and chicken adobo in her mouth. She held up her hand to let her mom know she was just chewing her food.

'I don't know,' Sarah said after taking a sip of water, 'Maybe I'll hang out with Miguel.'

'Did I hear someone say my name?' Miguel said, entering the dining room from the kitchen. Sarah loved her brother to bits. She would have hugged him, except he was covered with sweat.

'Where have you been?' Sarah asked.

'While you were sleeping off the day, I went biking!' Miguel loved to bike. His mountain bike was his one treasured possession, well, next to the computer. Sarah admired how athletic her baby brother was.

'Want to catch a movie?' she asked Miguel. That was a guaranteed way to make sure he would have no excuses. She saw his face light up. That was answer enough for Sarah.

Sarah loved how having a job gave her extra money for treats like new clothes for her mom and watching a movie with Miguel. Her mom didn't have a steady job and relied strictly on what their dad gave them on a monthly basis. Sarah hated her dad. She hadn't talked to him in years. He'd tried several times to reach out to her through her mom, but ever since he left the family home, she just couldn't bring herself to forgive him. They had once been so close and his separation from her mom had devastated her. She sealed him off from her life so he couldn't hurt her like that again. She couldn't deny, though, that he had stuck to his commitment to keep her family clothed and fed. She was grateful that her dad was paying for Miguel's education. So, Sarah saw it as her job to give her family the extras that they could indulge in once in a while, movies for Miguel, salon treats for her mom.

'What? I'm not invited?' her mom said. Even if her mom had put on her hurt face, Sarah knew that her mom loved it when she and Miguel took time to have bonding moments.

'Nope. It's a date. Moms not allowed.'

Her mom threw up her hands in mock despair.

'You better clean up right now, Miguel, or I might change my mind,' Sarah said.

'Taking a shower right now, Ate!' Miguel called out, racing to his room.

'Thanks, Sarah,' her mom kissed her. With no kids to worry about, her mom could go finish whatever project she was working on.

As Sarah got dressed for her movie date, she got another text message. This time from Anya: *Psst. Any updates?* Sarah laughed. Anya and Benito were a tag team today. Sarah texted back: *I am totally fine. Didn't you get the update from Benito? Out on a movie date with my bro. Do not disturb.*

'Ate, the movie is in forty-five minutes. Let's go!' Miguel was at the door. They commuted to the mall and decided to watch an action flick this time. They finished a bucket of popcorn between the two of them. Sarah was glad that Miguel had fun.

'Where do you want to eat?' Sarah asked Miguel.

'Somewhere quiet?'

'What? I thought you'd want a sports bar with some baby back ribs!' Sarah teased.

'I want to talk.'

'Uh-oh. Girl problems?'

'No, Ate. Your boy problems. I heard you crying.'

Sarah sighed.

They still chose to go to the sports bar with the baby back ribs but they settled for a corner table where they could talk in peace. Sarah realized that her break-up had affected Miguel too. She and Pete were together for six years. And in that time, Pete *did* become Miguel's older brother. It wasn't fair that Pete's relationship with Miguel would have to suffer because of the break-up, but that's what break-ups did.

'I'm sorry about what happened,' Miguel said.

'It's okay, Miguel. These things happen. I should have explained it to you better. I'm sorry. I was only thinking about myself.'

'Don't say that, Ate. You always put other people ahead of yourself. I just don't understand why Kuya Pete would break up with you.'

'I haven't been a good girlfriend.' Sarah was surprised about how easily that rolled off her tongue. It was something she could never have admitted to Pete.

'I don't believe that.' Miguel frowned.

Sarah thought it was sweet that Miguel was defending her. She swept the bangs off his forehead and looked him in the eyes. 'Well, you're not Pete.'

'You're the perfect girlfriend, Ate. Doesn't he realize that he's made a huge mistake?'

'Wow, when did you become so smart?' Sarah smiled slightly. 'But I'm not as perfect as you think. I've made my share of mistakes too. You know I'm such a workaholic. I just couldn't devote enough time to my relationship with Pete, especially after I got promoted.'

'But that's part of who you are. Why couldn't he wait for you to get used to it?'

'People change, Miguel. I guess Pete just couldn't wait for me to adjust.'

'He doesn't deserve you.'

Sarah ruffled her younger brother's hair. She couldn't say anything because what he said made her choke up.

Miguel's face lit up. 'Why don't you go biking with me?'

'I don't have a bike!'

'Well, you can always get one. You know what, Ate, you'll love the blog called *Maverick Marley*. It's run by this girl called Marley de Dios and she rides with my bike group sometimes. You should check it out.'

'Hmm. I'll think about it.' She honestly didn't feel up to it, but she thought of her spending yet another day moping in bed. Maybe getting outside would be good for her.

CHAPTER 3

Sarah stared at the picture on her screen for a while. The young woman in the picture had a gorgeous tan, a muscular physique, braided brown hair, and a big, confident smile. Sarah had taken her younger brother's advice to heart, and she was looking at Marley's profile. Marley wore a helmet, a pair of biking shades, and was sitting atop a mountain bike. The shot was taken on what looked like a mountain trail. Sarah felt both admiration and envy. She clicked on the 'follow' button at the bottom of the picture. *What would it take to have adventures like Marley?*

'Sarah, are you free for a few minutes?' Donna asked. Donna was her group manager.

'Sure!' Sarah replied, 'Do you want to talk in your cube?'

'Nope. Here is fine.' They weren't due for a status report meeting yet but Sarah did want to talk to Donna about why Richard, her client firm's rep, hadn't been in communication with her for a while. 'I just wanted you to know that there will be a general assembly tomorrow evening at the start of your shift. Please make sure that your whole team is there.'

'Okay, I'll do that, Donna.'

'I sent out an email already, but tell your team face to face so that no one misses the email. That's it.'

'Got it! By the way, I'm a bit worried that I haven't been getting any replies from Richard of MedNet lately. Has he been in touch with you?' Sarah was a stickler for sending status updates to her client. Usually, Richard acknowledged her emails, but not lately.

Sarah noticed that Donna hesitated for a moment. 'Maybe he's just on leave. I'll make sure to follow up with him.'

'Thanks, Donna.'

Sarah had a niggling feeling about the general assembly. But she quickly dismissed it. What should she have been worried about? She was meeting her quota.

'Finally!' Anya said as she gave Sarah a bear hug. 'How could you hole yourself up like that for a week?'

'I was depressed, okay? I'm fine now.' She heard Benito laugh.

'No one recovers from heartbreak in just a week,' Benito said, 'and that's from experience.'

Sarah was glad that Anya convinced her to meet up at their favourite 24/7 bar in the Ortigas area.

'Seriously, Sarah, how are you?' Anya asked.

'Let's order drinks first.'

'Now that's the spirit!' Benito said. He took care of ordering their drinks.

'I'm so touched that you guys are willing to drink early in the morning for me.'

'Anything for you, Sarah,' Anya replied.

Sarah, Anya, and Benito were best friends. They grew up together as neighbours in Marikina. They didn't all live on the same street any more, but they always had each other's backs, even managing to be schoolmates in the same college. They were very different from each other, but they all balanced each other out.

Anya was the free spirit, the artist. She worked at an ad agency as a copywriter, and they didn't mind the streaks of purple in her hair. They encouraged it. Benito was the wild one and the joker. He worked at his family's real estate company. He was the COO. Anya and Sarah joked about how it meant 'child of owner'. Sarah was the nerd and the steady anchor. Their little clique had grown when Pete became Sarah's boyfriend in college. Benito kept changing girlfriends, so they hardly counted as part of the group. It was Pete who became the fourth person in the group. And now, Pete was out of the picture. Just like the situation with Miguel, Sarah felt awful that Anya and Benito had lost a friend. But she was still grateful that she could turn to them in the aftermath of her break-up.

'First round on me. Mojitos for everyone,' Benito said as he gave each of them a cold glass overflowing with mint leaves and lime. 'Drink up.'

'I'm actually more worried about Miguel,' Sarah said after gulping down some of her mojito. 'He looked up to Pete.'

'Miguel will be fine. He has a lot of friends. Plus, he still has me,' Benito said.

That was true. Whenever Benito was at her house, he and Miguel, too, hung out a lot. Ever since his last break-up with his model girlfriend three months ago, Benito was hanging out more often at Sarah's place. Well, except for her one-week 'mourning' period.

'Do you want to start from the beginning?' Anya asked.

'No, Anya, I'd rather not,' Sarah said. All of a sudden, she couldn't stop her tears. *How do you start from the beginning after six years together? How do you start from the beginning when it all ended in a betrayal?*

Benito just kept handing her tissues. Both Anya and Benito were quiet. They waited for her to catch her breath.

'All I can say is that after six years together, I didn't expect Pete to cheat on me.'

Benito's eyes widened, 'He did what?' Anya put a restraining hand on Benito's hand that had curled into a fist.

'He claimed that it wasn't technically cheating . . .' Sarah started to explain.

'Well, let's see him define anything technically after I've broken his nose,' Benito said, gritting his teeth.

'Benito, it's all over. No one has to go break anyone's nose. I'm glad he did what he did. That way, I didn't have to stay, only to regret it later on.'

'You're right, Sarah,' Anya said as she gave Sarah's arm a squeeze.

'He claimed that I wasn't paying attention to him since my promotion. And you know what? I don't blame him,' Sarah confessed.

'That's a lot of bull,' Benito said, 'he could have resolved that a hundred other ways. It's no excuse to cheat on you.'

'That's actually what I told him,' Sarah said, 'and that's what made it easier for me to accept that it was over. I drew the line. There was just nothing else to discuss.'

'You did the right thing, Sarah,' Anya replied, 'but you can't get over this on your own. We're here for you.'

'I'm glad you guys have my back.'

After a couple more drinks and Pete-bashing, which Sarah completely did not mind, she took out her phone to show Anya and Benito the blog of Maverick Marley.

'What do you think?' Sarah asked.

'I think we're birds of the same feather. I like this Marley,' Anya said.

'Is it safe for her to be travelling alone?' Benito asked.

'Jeez, Benito, what century do you think we're living in?' Anya retorted.

'Really, Benito? I think she's having the time of her life. I'm actually thinking of doing what she's doing,' Sarah said.

'Girls, I'm not being a chauvinist. I was asking a serious question.'

'I don't think she travels by herself *all* the time,' Sarah said.

'Wait, wait, wait. What is wrong with travelling by yourself in the first place? Benito, it's that kind of question that is all kinds of chauvinistic,' Anya added.

'No chauvinism intended!' Benito said, raising his hands in the air in mock defeat.

'So, you're planning to travel?' Anya asked Sarah.

Interesting question. Sarah actually started feeling excited over the prospect.

'I don't have the luxury of time right now,' Sarah said, 'but I wouldn't mind planning for it sometime next year.'

'Why don't you start planning now? Seat sales aren't easy to catch when they're too close to your departure dates,' Anya said.

'Okay, I will. But first, I think I want to meet Marley.'

'Me too,' Benito said, 'she's cute.'

'Ugh, Benito!' Sarah groaned.

Actually, it wasn't far-fetched that Benito could date a girl like Marley in a snap. Beautiful girls fell for Benito all the time. He could never be without a girlfriend because as soon as he dumped a girl (or was dumped), another girl was lining up to be his girlfriend. Sarah looked at her friend in an assessing way for once. He had all the qualities of a 'catch': a buff body (Benito did not scrimp on gym time), rugged good looks (stubbly square jaw did not exactly appeal to Sarah but, apparently, it appealed to a lot of other girls), and an infectious sense of humour. All of that plus the fact that he drove a BMW made him an eligible bachelor if he weren't so serially monogamous. It was a miracle that after he broke up with Gia, the model, three months ago, he was still single. Sarah snapped out of her weird train of thought. Did she have too many mojitos? She took a sip of water, but she was still feeling a bit fuzzy. One thing was clear to her: she had better get to Marley before Benito did.

'How are you feeling now, Sarah?' Benito asked, hours later. He looked concerned.

'I'm a bit buzzed. Thank you, guys. That was fun!'

'I'm driving you home,' Benito said.

'I'm fine.'

'No, you're not,' Anya and Benito said together.

Sarah laughed.

'I'm driving you home,' Benito repeated. Anya nodded. He took Sarah's handbag and held her elbow. She leaned on his shoulder. It felt nice to have her head nestled there.

Anya kissed her goodbye. She needed to catch a ride to a meeting. 'Text me when you get her home,' she told Benito.

Benito put his arm around Sarah, and they headed out the door.

A waiter caught up with them. 'Sir,' he called out. 'Your girlfriend left her phone on the table.' He handed Benito Sarah's phone.

'I'm not his girlfriend,' she protested.

'Thank you,' Benito smiled at the waiter. He tightened his grip on her shoulder. 'C'mon, girlfriend.'

She found it amusing that he enjoyed the waiter's mistake. 'Alright, boyfriend,' and she put her arm around his waist.

CHAPTER 4

At 10 p.m. sharp, Sarah gathered her team of twelve (including those scheduled for other shifts) and they proceeded to one of the larger training rooms on their floor. The seats were arranged classroom style and there was a microphone in front of the rows of chairs as well as in the aisle. Behind the chairs were a series of office tables arranged in rows. Donna was already there. Albert, their HR director, followed Donna to the side of the room. Albert was usually jolly and smiling. With his big-boned frame and round cheeks, he was a cheerful presence at the office. Tonight, though, he looked sombre. Sarah tried to guess what the general assembly was going to be about. Were they going to get a new client? Was there going to be a reorganization? In the two years that she'd worked for TechConnect, she'd experienced similar general assemblies in the past and it was usually to coordinate big changes like new accounts or merging teams.

Donna went up to the mike facing the assembly and said, 'Good evening, everyone. I'm sure you're all wondering why we're gathered here.' There were some nods.

'Let me start by giving you some news first. MedNet has dissolved as a company, and they are no longer our clients.'

The room was eerily quiet. Sarah heard a few gasps but nothing more than that.

'This has business implications on the entire support team of the client,' Donna continued. 'We're all here today because we need to discuss your options. Albert, our HR Director, will take you through the process.'

The process? What was this, a conveyor belt? Sarah felt her heart palpitate. There was no way this was going to end well.

'Team,' Albert addressed the small group, 'our vacancies are currently filled. As much as we would have wanted to absorb this unit into other operations, we have very limited options. This was a very tough choice. But we want to be transparent. This unit has been assessed as redundant.'

Who assessed? Sarah felt blood rush to her head. She raised her hand. *This is not happening.*

'Yes, Sarah,' Albert said.

'Are we being retrenched?' Sarah asked. She knew that her voice had gone up a notch. But she didn't care. This was her life. This was her job. Did they just say that they were taking it away from her?

'That's a good question. I was just getting there,' Albert said, 'Can we take it step by step?'

Sarah took her seat.

'What I was saying,' Albert continued, a little bit flustered this time, 'was that the team was found to be redundant, and since you cannot fill other vacancies, because currently there are none, we have prepared separation packages for you, and we will make sure that we support you through your job applications.'

No, no, no! Sarah looked around, and everyone was looking shocked, confused. Some of her team members were already crying. Some of them looked at *her* as if she had some kind of answer for them. She had none. She realized then that she was also crying along with them.

Donna was back at the mike. 'Everyone, please calm down. We haven't explained the next steps yet.'

'Don't we have any say in this?' Sarah once again asked. This time she didn't raise her hand, but she went straight to the mike in the aisle. She was the team leader, after all. She needed to voice out what her entire team was thinking in their heads. To Sarah, this wasn't just a job she was proud of. This was her way of supporting her family. She had team members who were married. Some of them had kids. What would happen to them?

'We did go through as many scenarios as possible. This is really the last resort.'

At that point, several HR associates entered the room with stacks of folders and started sitting at the tables at the back of the assembly.

Albert took over the mike again, 'We have prepared generous separation packages for you, and we will be sitting down with each of you to explain them. Sarah, please follow me.'

Albert stationed himself at one of the tables and pulled a chair for Sarah to sit on. *How could Albert be so calm?* First, Pete left her. And ironically, the reason for Pete's defection, her 'precious' job, was also gone in what seemed like the blink of an eye. Why was the world ending? What did she do wrong?

'Albert, we were hitting our numbers,' Sarah said, trying to keep her voice down. Inside, she panicked for her entire team, but on the outside, she kept the desperation out of her voice. 'Why this?'

'Sarah, this is really painful for me too. But it has nothing to do with the numbers you were doing. This has nothing to do with how good you are as a team leader.'

'How could you say that? Didn't you just tell me we've been fired?'

'Sarah, redundancy is different from being fired. There isn't a more competent team leader than you. However, a business unit has just dissolved. We have to deal with the consequences.'

'No,' Sarah said through her tears, '*I* have to deal with the consequences. All of my team members too.'

'I'm really sorry.'

Albert waited for Sarah to wipe her tears and blow her nose.

'Sarah, this is your separation package,' he said, indicating a piece of paper in the folder he held open for her. It is two times your monthly salary for every year that you have been employed with TechConnect. This amount is tax-exempt because the cause of the separation is beyond your control.'

Sarah paused and did the math.

'We will be helping you with letters of recommendation—' Sarah didn't really hear the rest of what he was saying because an idea hit her right there in the middle of her retrenchment. Maybe this was an opportunity to start something different, do something different. She just wasn't sure what it was yet.

'Sarah? Are you okay? Do you need a glass of water?' Albert said.

'No, I'm not okay. This is a lot to absorb, Albert.'

'I was just explaining to you that we will be helping you and your team find jobs elsewhere and we will make sure to support you by giving letters of recommendation.'

'Okay, Albert. Where do I sign?' Once reality hit her, Sarah dealt with the situation the same way she dealt with Pete: quickly. There was nothing to fight for, it seemed, so it was better that this was done quickly and cleanly.

They were told that they had until the end of the week to clear out their things from their work desks. But who would want to prolong the agony? Sarah wanted to get out as soon as possible. She just dreaded giving the news to her mom. How would she explain it? *Mom, I lost my job. But, don't worry, I wasn't fired or anything. I just wasn't necessary any more.* It sounded like a bad joke. On her way out of the training room, she couldn't even look at Donna. Sarah was just too upset. She couldn't bear the thought of facing her team when they got to their work areas.

This. Will. Not. Kill. Me. She kept saying it in her head, just to stay sane.

CHAPTER 5

Sarah sat at her colour-coordinated desk, the space a reflection of her orderly, Type-A personality. Her laptop was open to a detailed spreadsheet labelled 'Life Plan 2.0'. The original 'Life Plan' sheet had gone awry. Behind her, a minimalist wall clock's hands moved in precise symmetry, ticking away seconds as if measuring out the fragments of her old life. The room was silent except for the subtle tap-tap-tap of Sarah typing away, updating her résumé. Her vision board, filled with intentions and ambitions—career goals, a life with Pete in their dream condo, and projected personal milestones (another promotion)—was a painful reminder of how all her plans had been thwarted. The glow of her laptop screen cast sharp shadows across her face. She sat, unblinking, her fingers a testament to her resolve, each click a step towards a new job. Her meticulous spreadsheet of potential employers, job postings, and application deadlines spanned several tabs—a sea of opportunity she intended to navigate with her typical precision.

'Honey, can I come in?' Helen, her mother, asked, knocking softly on the closed door.

'Come in, Ma,' Sarah replied, barely raising her eyes from the screen.

Helen walked in, the concern in her eyes deepening as she took in her daughter's singular focus. 'You've been in here since morning. You haven't even had lunch.'

'I had a protein bar. I have no time for sit-down meals right now,' Sarah said, her fingers not pausing over the keyboard.

Helen sighed. 'You're acting like a job-hunting machine. You've just been laid off and you and Pete just broke up. Shouldn't you take some time to . . . process?'

Sarah glanced at her mother, her face stoic. 'I've scheduled emotional processing time from 7.45 to 8.00 p.m. Right now, I have other things to deal with.'

'But, honey—'

'Ma, please, I need to focus. I can't afford to waste time. I need to plan my next move.'

'Sarah, you've been at this since dawn,' Helen said, her voice laced with concern. 'You haven't taken a moment for yourself. Everyone needs to breathe, even you.'

Sarah's posture remained unwavering, her gaze fixed. 'Breathing doesn't land you a job. Being proactive does.'

Miguel burst into the room, brandishing his phone like a treasure hunter who'd just struck gold. 'Ate, I have news! It's epic!'

Sarah shot him a look of irritation. 'I'm busy.'

'Busy being a workaholic? Ma's right, Ate. You need to take a break.'

Sarah saved her document, gritting her teeth. 'I can't afford a "break".'

'Ate, trust me. I've set up a meeting for you and Marley. As in Maverick Marley! You remember her, right? The blogger I follow? The one who goes on some of our group's bike trips? The one who's always travelling to some exotic destination and talking about living life to the fullest?'

Sarah sighed. 'I don't have time for this. I have to find a job.'

'That's exactly why you should meet her. You never know, you might get some new ideas from her or something.'

Sarah was torn. She didn't want to let her brother down. He was so excited and so sincere.

'I'll think about it, okay? I promise.'

It wasn't the answer Miguel was expecting.

In the doorway, Miguel shuffled his feet, his youthful face pinched with worry. 'Ate, you haven't even laughed since . . . you know,' he mumbled. 'It's kinda scary.'

Sarah finally turned, offering a practised smile that didn't quite reach her eyes. 'Don't worry about me. I've got this under control.'

Helen exchanged a look with Miguel, her eyes signalling a silent conversation they had shared too often these past few days. She stepped forward, her hand reaching out to brush Sarah's arm. 'You're more than a well-oiled machine. It's okay to feel, to take a break.'

But Sarah was already turning back to her screen, her fingers resuming their dance across the keys. 'Breaks are for people who have the luxury of time. I don't,' she stated, her voice as steady as the rhythm of her typing.

Her mother's frown deepened, but she nodded, leaving Sarah to her relentless pursuit. As she closed the door, the soft click sounded like a goodbye to normalcy.

That evening, Sarah heard the doorbell ring. She waited for someone to get the door, but it seemed like both her mom and her brother had gone deaf. The doorbell rang again. She hesitated before finally prying herself away from her desk. Opening the door, she found Anya and Benito standing outside, armed with a box of pastries and a board game.

'We're staging an intervention,' Anya announced, walking past Sarah into the house.

'A what now?'

Benito followed Anya inside. 'Your mom called us, Sarah. Said you're on the brink of turning into a hermit or a robot, or maybe both.'

Sarah sighed as they settled into the living room. 'I can't just pause life to have fun, guys.'

'But you can pause for friendship, can't you?' Benito looked at her, a gentle sincerity in his eyes.

'We're worried about you, Sarah,' Anya added.

'One game. I can play one game,' Sarah finally conceded.

As they played, Sarah's mind wasn't fully present. Her moves were calculated but joyless, a series of auto-pilot decisions. She was the first to declare victory, but it felt like anything but a win.

'You won, Sarah,' Anya said softly.

'Did I?' Sarah looked at her friends, her gaze falling on Benito, who seemed extra concerned. 'Maybe I've been winning all the wrong battles.'

Benito looked up, his eyes meeting hers, then quickly looking away. 'Or maybe you've been fighting them in the wrong way.'

Anya exchanged a glance with Benito, her eyes signalling their shared mission. 'Your mom's worried about you,' she said gently. 'We all are. There's more to life than the perfect job.'

'And what would that be?' Sarah's voice held an edge of defensiveness, but also a hint of genuine curiosity.

'You used to love photography,' Benito reminded her. 'Remember those weekends we spent chasing the perfect shot?'

Sarah's expression softened at the memory, but she was quick to be on guard again. 'That was before. I need stability, not snapshots.'

Anya moved to sit beside Sarah on the couch, her presence warm and reassuring. 'Stability will come. But you don't have to chase it down like it's the last bus of the night.'

Sarah looked between her two friends, the relentless drive that fuelled her suddenly faltering in the face of their concern. 'I just . . . I can't fall behind.'

'You're not behind, you're ahead of everyone else,' Benito said, his voice kind. 'But even the best runners need to catch their breath.'

Sarah's gaze fell to her hands, the tension in her shoulders easing as she considered their words. Her world, once narrowed to the confines of job descriptions and application forms, seemed to widen just a fraction.

Miguel burst back into the room, his excitement palpable. 'So, have you decided? Are you okay with meeting Marley? She's been waiting for me to confirm.'

'I don't know . . .' Sarah hesitated.

'Ate, please,' Miguel implored. 'You used to be so lively before . . . before everything got so serious. Marley's all about living in the moment and grabbing life with both hands.'

Helen, who had quietly entered the room, added, 'Sarah, honey, I think this could be good for you. A little break, some fresh air, new perspectives.'

The unspoken words—'like you used to'—hung in the air.

Sarah looked at her brother, his eagerness a stark contrast to the calculated world she had wrapped around herself. She felt Helen's hopeful gaze and saw the soft encouragement in Anya and Benito's eyes.

Sarah sighed, a reluctant smile forming on her lips. 'Alright. I'll go.'

'Really?' He looked surprised but ecstatic.

Miguel's cheer filled the room, and even Sarah couldn't help but be affected by his infectious optimism. As her family and friends rallied around her, for the first time in weeks, her own laugh mingled with theirs, genuine and unburdened.

'Yeah,' Sarah replied. 'What's the worst that could happen? I lose a few hours that I could have spent job-hunting?'

'Or you gain a new friend,' Miguel suggested, grinning.

When her family and friends finally left her alone, Sarah returned to her desk, looking at her spreadsheet and the vision board hanging on the wall. For the first time, they seemed like relics of a life she was no longer completely sure of. She hesitated, then closed her laptop.

With a new-found uncertainty, Sarah picked up a marker and wrote 'Maverick Marley' on her wall calendar. It was a small, asymmetrical glitch in her meticulously symmetrical world, but maybe, just maybe, that was exactly what she needed. It felt like the rug had been pulled from under her. Two losses, one after the other, were a shock to her system.

Outwardly, she felt that she needed to show her family and her friends that she was strong. She didn't want them to feel sorry for her. But, inside, her world was crumbling. More than anything, she felt scared. She'd always known what to do. When her mom had been separated from her dad, there were weeks when Helen failed to function. She was in bed most of the time. Sarah had learned to fend for herself. She learned to cook on her own, relying on tutorial videos on the internet, even while her heart was breaking too. And here she was again, not enough. She wasn't enough of a daughter for her dad to stay. She wasn't enough of a girlfriend for Pete to stay. She wasn't enough of a professional to keep her job. What would it take to just be content and happy?

She returned to her desk, opened a blank document, and began typing, her words now guided by more than just deadlines and goals. The clock struck 7.45 p.m., her 'scheduled emotional processing time', but for once, Sarah continued to type, breaking her own rules and venturing into uncharted territories of spontaneity. It wasn't a surrender to her circumstances but an acknowledgment that, perhaps, amidst the relentless pursuit of her plans, life was happening—and she was finally allowing herself a moment to live it.

As the clock ticked away, Sarah felt an unusual but welcome lightness in her chest. The grief was still there, but slightly alleviated by new plans to take a break. Maybe it was okay to be a little unpredictable, to give herself permission to breathe, to live outside the spreadsheet. Tomorrow would be a new day, unpredictable and challenging, but for the first time, Sarah felt truly ready to meet it.

Steady Sarah might just be ready for some new adventures.

CHAPTER 6

Sarah woke up to the late morning sunlight brightening her room. She hadn't experienced sleeping in until late on a weekday in a very long time. She took a moment to just savour the luxury of it. Beside her was her mom, still asleep.

For the past few weeks, Sarah hadn't been able to sleep by herself. She had started sharing her mom's bed so she could force herself to get some rest. She just needed her mom beside her. Even when they weren't talking, she felt comforted by her presence. Could she move out to a condo and live by herself? She thought she was ready. But maybe not right now.

Sarah gently pushed aside the blanket and got out of bed, making sure she didn't wake her mom. She went to the kitchen to make herself some coffee, and then started making breakfast. Because they'd been on a limited budget since forever, her mom had taken care of all their needs without ever hiring help. Both she and Miguel learned how to cook, do the laundry, and clean the house from their mom. Since she lost her job, Sarah had taken on cooking breakfast as a treat for her mom. She wanted to be useful, to keep herself busy, and to let her mom sleep in, for once.

It was also a special day for Sarah. Through Miguel, she'd arranged to meet with Marley de Dios, the woman behind the travel blog, *Maverick Marley*. She decided to take a break from the stress of writing up applications and sending out her résumé. She wanted to know what it took to lead a life of adventure like Marley's.

'Something smells good,' her mom said, smiling.

'Sit down, Ma. Just relax. I'll take care of everything.'

'No, I'll take care of setting the table,' her mom said as she headed straight to the dish rack. Miguel beat her to it, though.

'Good morning, Ma,' he said, 'Just sit down. Ate and I will get breakfast for you.'

'I have the sweetest children,' their mom said.

After a few minutes, they were all seated at the table eating corned beef, fried rice, and omelette, with cups of steaming coffee.

'I'm really excited for you, Ate. Where are you meeting Marley?' Miguel asked.

'I'm meeting her at the Blue Coast shopping centre. We're having lunch.'

'Cool! Say hi to her for me, okay? She's really fun to talk to.'

Someone rang the doorbell. It was Miguel's bus service. He kissed Sarah and their mom, grabbed his lunch bag on the kitchen counter, and rushed out the door.

'How are you doing, anak?' her mom asked. Sarah knew that her mom didn't mean to pressure her, but she felt pressured just the same.

'Still no word from earlier submissions.'

'I'm not talking about your job hunt. I'm talking about *you*. How are *you*?'

'I'll get myself together soon. I promise.'

'I talked to your dad.'

This was a trigger point between her and her mom.

'Why?'

'I told him the situation. He's still your father, Sarah.'

'I know that you're worried about the money, Ma. But why did you have to involve him?'

'Sarah, it's not about the money—'

'Yeah, it's never supposed to be about the money but it's always the elephant in the room, isn't it?'

'Sarah, your dad cares about you.'

'Oh please. He left us, Ma. He left us!' Sarah couldn't help raising her voice. How could her mother be such a *doormat*?

'He took care of us. He didn't let go of that responsibility.'

'Well, I don't consider him my father.'

'Sarah, please don't say that.'

'He would have been here if he really cared. But no, he pays us. He pays us so he doesn't have to feel guilty.'

'It's not like that!'

'Whatever, Ma. I don't want to talk about him. Let's not talk about him.' Sarah felt tears coming on but she wouldn't let them fall.

'He's giving us extra allowance while you're looking for a job.'

That was it. Sarah stood up.

'Ma, I love you. But *this*, I can't stand this. I'm going to my room now,' she said. She hated it. She hated leaving her mom at the dining table when, just a few minutes ago, they were all laughing and enjoying breakfast together.

But once again, Jorge Silvestre managed to ruin the day without actually being present. As far as Sarah was concerned, he could go to hell.

Despite feeling bad about her earlier conversation with her mom, Sarah headed out to Blue Coast in high spirits. She didn't know exactly what to expect and sipped her tea while waiting for Marley. Her phone beeped: *I'll be there in a few minutes. Wearing a pink tank top. See you.*

Sarah knew it was Marley from her blog photos. In person, Marley was even prettier. And buff, too! She was carrying only her bike helmet.

'Marley!' she called out, motioning to her booth at the coffee shop. Marley waved at her and walked over.

'Hi, Sarah! It's great to finally meet you,' Marley said. Sarah didn't expect such a low voice. She was instantly in awe of her. They shook hands.

'Did you actually bike here?' Sarah asked.

'Yes! I rode from Katipunan Avenue. It wasn't such a long ride.'

'Wow! Wait. What do you want to order? It's my treat. I'm the one who invited you over,' Sarah said. Marley said thanks and ordered a salad with shrimp and a glass of pineapple juice. Sarah felt guilty for ordering a creamy pasta *and* chicken chops but she just wanted to enjoy the day. No diets.

'Miguel can't stop talking about you,' Sarah said.

'Your brother is a great kid. He's really patient and he works out seriously so he can improve his skill biking uphill.'

'Yup. That's Miguel,' Sarah said proudly.

'So, how can I help you?'

'I just really wanted to find out how you do it, how you go on adventures. Do you do it while you're working at a full-time job?'

Marley laughed. 'Yes, I have a job but not a regular nine-to-five job. I'm a training consultant so I get to choose my hours.'

'Wow!'

'There are perks. But then again, there are also stress points. I have to keep sourcing new contracts and working with partners. As for my adventures, I really plan them ahead so I can get the best deals.'

'So, you plan them like projects?'

'You could say that. I made a choice. I decided that I wouldn't buy a lot of stuff so I could save for experiences like travel. Since I have a limited travel budget, I really have to make it a project so I can get the most out of what I can afford.'

'Isn't there a lot of risk involved when you're self-employed?'

Marley smiled. 'Sometimes we have to take risks to truly find ourselves.'

Sarah made a mental note to memorize that insight. Sarah observed how healthy and full of life Marley was. She was so fit, tan, and glowing. She caught herself envying Marley. As she dug into her pasta, she wondered again if she should have ordered a salad. Marley seemed to be enjoying hers as she took sips of her chilled juice.

'How did you start?'

'Hmm. Before my consulting stint, I used to work for an NGO. I got to travel around the Philippines because of my job. And it was a really great experience for me. I didn't want to stop just because it wasn't my job any more.'

Sarah was fascinated by what Marley shared. Her mind was going on overdrive with possibilities.

'Okay,' Sarah continued, 'I wanted to make a request. I don't know if this is something that you're willing to do but I want to ask anyway.'

'What is it?'

'Can I be your apprentice? At least for one or two things that you're planning. I want to learn.'

'Sarah,' Marley said, laughing, 'you're the first person who's actually asked. I've had marketing requests and tie-up proposals but no one's ever asked to apprentice.'

'I'm serious, Marley. I actually don't have a job right now and I've saved some money. I'd really love to go on an adventure with you.'

Marley looked thoughtful. 'Hmm . . .' She gave Sarah a discerning look.

It gave Sarah the jitters.

'Is this something you can really commit to? Maybe you're just bored right now because you don't have a job. You have to be fit to go hiking and biking. How's your health and stamina?'

Sarah was surprised by Marley's question. It sounded like an interview.

'I have to be honest. I'm really not that fit right now. My job was on the sedentary side. But I won't let that stop me. I'll train.' Sarah promised.

'Okay, let's see,' Marley said. She took out her phone and checked her calendar. 'I haven't scheduled anything major in the near future. But I do have a couple of trips not far from the city that you might want to join.'

'Consider me signed up,' Sarah replied.

'Okay, I have a trip to Batlag Falls two weeks from now. You can come along. I'll check with my biking group if the trip to Santa Ines is pushing through. You can join that one too, but only if you seriously work out before the trip. Otherwise, you might delay the whole group.'

'I promise to prepare ahead. Marley, you are a godsend,' Sarah said.

'Do you know how to bike?'

'Yes, I do. But I'll have to borrow my brother's mountain bike.'

'Yup, a mountain bike would be best. I suggest you start practising on it already. Given that you're more used to office life, you need to get on a workout programme. You need to build stamina. It works two ways. First, you need to get used to more rigorous activity and build some muscle, and, second, you need to match it with clean eating.'

'Clean eating? Does it mean I have to keep eating salads?' Sarah asked, indicating Marley's salad.

'No,' Marley laughed, 'it doesn't mean you have to keep eating salads. Clean eating just means eating food that's as close to its natural state as possible. That means no processed food, like hotdogs. Avoid eating at fast food restaurants if you can. Don't worry, I'll send you a programme.'

Workout? Clean eating? What did she just get into?

'Okay. I'll do whatever it takes.'

'That's the spirit!'

She had no idea where Batlag Falls was, but she already made up her mind that she was going. Sarah knew that this was the start of a new friendship and a new chapter in her story.

CHAPTER 7

Sarah sat at her desk, her eyes fixed on her laptop's glowing screen. She had strategically minimized her job-hunting tabs—LinkedIn, Jobstreet, and Glassdoor—guilt gnawing at her as she hesitantly clicked on Facebook. Her fingers trembled as she typed in Pete's name. She momentarily looked up. Pete's face was smiling back at her from the framed photograph on her desk. She hadn't had time to take it down and replace it. But replace it with what? Honestly, she missed him.

The promotion had been a double-edged sword, cutting deep into her relationship with Pete. He accused her of being too immersed in her work, of scaling the corporate ladder while forgetting to tend to their relationship. And maybe he was right; perhaps she had been too consumed with reports and presentations, but wasn't it all for their future?

Despite the hurt, Sarah yearned for the times when life was as predictable as Pete's choice of ties—striped for meetings, solid for dates. That was Pete, with that polished smile, looking dapper in a casual shirt and jeans. Predictable Pete. She scrolled through his photos—here he was at a corporate seminar, presenting some bar graphs; and another was at his sister's graduation, a family guy to the core.

She had not unfriended and unfollowed him yet; her finger had hovered over those buttons many times, but each time, her resolve crumbled.

The photos on the screen painted a portrait of Pete's new life without her. There he was at a karaoke outing, his head thrown back in laughter, a microphone clutched like a trophy in his hand. Now, scrolling through Pete's recent history, Sarah saw him seemingly embracing more of these moments without her. It stung. She realized that their togetherness might have been a mutual safety net, one that held them from diving into life's vibrant chaos.

Then she saw a picture of just Pete and Joanna. They were both in a work setting but they were seated next to each other. They had big smiles on their faces. She knew Pete. He looked relaxed. More relaxed than she'd ever seen him. He looked happy.

She felt a pang of jealousy. There was an ease between Pete and Joanna that she and Pete had lost somewhere along the way.

She looked at Pete's smiling face and contemplated leaving a comment—a casual, friendly note that might bridge the distance between their separate worlds. But as she stared at the screen, her mind reminded her heart that this digital window into Pete's life was not hers to open any more.

'Ugh. Why am I doing this to myself?' she muttered, her eyes involuntarily welling up. 'Why did Pete do this to us?'

Two years ago

Sarah was visibly excited, her eyes sparkling. 'Pete, how about we take a road trip this weekend? We could visit that artsy town a couple of hours away. They have that food festival going on, and it could be fun to explore the local shops,' she said excitedly.

Pete looked puzzled. 'A road trip? On such short notice? What about our plans to see that new Marvel movie and go to our favourite Italian restaurant?'

'That's exactly why we should go. It's something different, something unplanned.' Sarah's voice was filled with an enthusiasm that wasn't mirrored in Pete's eyes.

'You know how much you love their carbonara, and I can't get enough of their tiramisu,' he said, trying to lure her back to their usual routine.

'You're so predictable,' she said, the excitement draining from her face.

Pete chuckled softly, his eyes meeting hers. 'You love me for my predictability, remember?'

That much was true, Sarah realized now. Predictability was something she had come to yearn for, especially after her parents separated.

But had she and Pete really been happy? They had settled into a routine. They finished each other's sentences. She considered him her best friend. But why hadn't she picked up on his sadness? He accused her of deprioritizing him. Had she counted on his patience too much?

A text notification from Anya snapped Sarah back to the present.

Anya: *Hey, everything alright?*

Sarah: *Taking a detour down memory lane, unfortunately.*

Anya: *Oh, going through the 'ex-files,' huh?*

Sarah chuckled, grateful for her friend's light-heartedness.

Sarah: *Yeah, something like that.*

She clicked back on Pete's profile and then saw it—a post quoting some business guru: *Predictability may feel comfortable, but it doesn't promote growth.*

Wow, Pete, the irony, she thought, feeling a shiver go down her spine.

A thought crossed her mind, strong and resolute: *I need to grow, just like Pete said. Maybe not in the way he's thinking, but in my own way.* She looked back at her journal entry. *Should I start a blog? Like Marley? Maybe.*

Her phone buzzed one more time, and Sarah's heart skipped a beat when she saw the unsaved number.

Unknown: *Hi Sarah, it's Pete. Can we talk?*

Her emotions soared and plummeted all at once. An adrenaline rush of anticipation and dread surged through her veins. She hesitated before replying.

Sarah: *Of course.*

Unknown: *I've been doing a lot of thinking. Can we catch up over coffee?*

Sarah felt the room closing in on her. She remembered the comfort of their routines, the security in Pete's predictability. But then Marley's words echoed in her mind: 'Sometimes we have to take risks to truly find ourselves.' She'd just been missing Pete earlier. And now, here he was, texting her. What did he want to say? Had he changed his mind? Did he want to get back together? Would it hurt all over again?

Sarah: *Meet you at the café outside my village in an hour?*

Unknown: *Thanks, Sarah. It means a lot to me.*

Would she regret seeing him? Maybe. All she knew in her heart was she needed to see him. What was she expecting, anyway? There was only one way to find out.

The café outside her village was really small. She didn't want to sit inside and have everyone hear their conversation, so she sat outside, under one of the canopied tables. She saw him before he saw her. She missed him. She missed seeing his face. She missed his smile. Why did they even break up? She took a deep breath so all her questions wouldn't show up so clearly on her face.

'Hey, Sarah.'

I've missed his voice. 'Hey,' it was all she could manage. There was an awkward pause. On a normal day, they'd have exchanged kisses on the cheek. But this was not a normal day.

'Let me get us some coffee first,' Pete said. Sarah nodded. Again, he didn't really need to ask her what she wanted. He already knew. While he was inside, she took more deep breaths. Just seeing him had raised her heartbeat. Would he tell her he made a mistake? She quashed that hope as quickly as it had appeared. Hadn't she just seen his pictures on Facebook? Hadn't he looked happy with Joanna?

Don't hope. Don't hope.

Pete set down the covered paper cups of coffee on the table and smiled. *God, that smile.*

'Thanks for meeting me. How have you been?'

Should I lie? 'It's not been the best. I got retrenched,' she said it so naturally. She was so used to telling Pete everything.

'I'm so sorry to hear that.' There was genuine concern in his voice. But no, there would be no big hug this time. She could feel it. He was different.

'I'll be fine.' There was the lie. 'What about you? How have you been?'

'Work's been fine. But I feel bad about the last time we met. I feel like we left a lot of things unsaid. I'm sorry if I came off as a defensive jerk. I didn't mean to.'

Sarah still loved Pete. She could feel it in her heart. She'd been angry at the time. They had both been tired. Was she still angry?

'But you're happier now, right? With Joanna?' She couldn't help herself. She didn't want to rile him. But she needed to know if it was really over for him, for them. She needed him to know that she'd seen the pictures. He looked away for a few seconds. And when he looked at her again, there were tears in his eyes. She wanted to reach for him. It was her first instinct. She had to stop herself.

'I've missed us being us, the way we used to be,' Pete said.

'Then, why didn't we talk about it, Pete? Why didn't you give us a chance?' This was what hurt her the most.

'Haven't you felt that we've grown apart?' Pete asked.

'I was just focused on something else. I didn't think we were growing apart.' She searched his face. She saw all the hurt there too.

'You're right, though, Sarah. I've been happier lately.'

'Are you together with her?'

'We're not officially together. Yet.'

'So, what? Are you asking for my permission or something?' She wanted to be angry again.

'No, nothing like that,' Pete said quickly, running his hands through his hair, a nervous tic that was familiar to her.

'You said you've been doing a lot of thinking. Why did you want to meet?'

'I wanted to apologize.'

'About what?'

'It wasn't your fault,' he said.

Sarah's eyes widened. She didn't expect him to admit this, but it wasn't enough for her. 'But it wasn't your fault, either?'

'It wasn't anyone's fault, Sarah. We're just different now.'

She wanted badly to retort, *No, you're the one who's different. You're the one who fell in love with someone else.* But she knew it wouldn't go anywhere.

Sarah realized that six years of being together couldn't undo Pete's falling in love with someone else.

I love you, Pete, but I've lost you.

This time, it was her turn to cry. She couldn't undo time. She couldn't undo *this*.

'I'm sorry for hurting you, Sarah.' Pete said, his eyes downcast.

'I'm sorry too.' Sarah attempted to wipe her tears with the palm of her hand, but Pete, ever the gentleman, handed her his handkerchief from his pocket.

'Can we still be friends?' *Could we?*

'I just can't answer that question right now.'

At home, Sarah broke down again. This time, though, she knew it was really over. Despite the grief and the finality, she also felt a sense of relief, a bittersweet emotion of ending one chapter to begin another.

In the stillness of her room, Sarah wrapped her arms around herself as if to hold together the pieces of a puzzle that were falling apart. The silence was her canvas, and on it, she projected the vivid colours of her memories with Pete—their laughter, their silences, their unspoken understanding that had once seemed unbreakable.

Yet here she was, in the aftermath of their break-up, wrestling with the temptation to reach back and grasp at the threads of a connection that had once defined her. Pete had moved on, not just in relationship but in spirit, embracing a spontaneity that he had never shown with her. It begged the question: Had she been the anchor that weighed down his adventurous side?

A draft of cold air whispered through the room, carrying with it the faint scent of cologne—Pete's cologne. It was enough to make her heart clench.

She imagined the sound of his voice, the predictable comfort of his 'hey' that had once been the start of so many of their conversations. Sarah closed her eyes, allowing herself to feel the full weight of her longing, the ache for the ease of their old rhythm.

But the silence spoke to her, filling the room with the truth that resounded louder than any conversation she could have with Pete. She knew she was growing. She realized that the comfort of predictability was also a barrier that kept her from dancing to her own beat.

Sarah opened her eyes, her decision settling in with a quiet finality. This was it. She would not disturb the delicate balance of letting go. Instead, she chose to embrace the silence, to listen to the voice within that had been drowned out by the noise of her longing. She added back Pete's name to her contacts. It had been useless to erase it anyway.

Sarah: *Please give me time, Pete. You're right, though. We're headed in different directions now.*

She hit send, her heart pounding in her chest.

Pete was typing. He paused. Finally, the text came.

Pete: *I get it. I wish you the best, Sarah.*

Sarah: *You too, Pete. Take care.*

Her thumb slid away from Pete's contact name, navigating instead to her own profile, to her own life that was waiting to be lived. She made a new post, a simple picture of the night sky from her balcony, stars scattered like silver dust against the velvet darkness. Her caption was a promise, to herself more than anyone else:

A promise to myself—to notice the stars when they're shining.

As she set her phone down, a sense of peace began to weave its way through the fabric of her being. She had chosen herself, chosen the uncertainty of new paths, and the adventure of finding what lay beyond the predictable horizon.

In her resolve, Sarah felt a new chapter stirring, ready to unfold with the first rays of the morning sun. It was time to chase the waterfalls of her own making, to discover the depths of her soul that had been waiting patiently beneath the still waters of Steady Sarah.

CHAPTER 8

In the next few days, Sarah continued with her job search, but she felt restless. She tossed and turned in her bed. Even though she had somehow resolved things with Pete, she still felt rudderless. She had gnawing questions about love, work, marriage, and her dad that haunted her.

Finally, Sarah gave up on sleep and quietly made her way to the kitchen. She found her mom there, sitting at the table, a dim light casting a soft glow on her face. Helen was holding a saucepan filled with hot chocolate, the aroma of tablea filling the room. Her hands moved with a quiet certainty as she dropped more chunks of tablea into the pot.

Helen looked up, and a small smile spread across her face. 'Couldn't sleep either?'

Sarah shook her head and joined her at the table. 'No, my mind is all over the place.'

'Lola said this was good for the soul,' Helen offered.

Sarah watched, tracing the patterns of steam curling up into the air. 'I need that drink,' she replied.

As they sipped their hot chocolate, the conversation flowed naturally. They talked about their shared love for reading. They laughed about something Miguel had done.

For a moment, it was just a mother and her daughter bonding in the quiet hours of the night.

They continued to sip the thick, dark chocolate in companionable silence, each lost in thought, until Sarah's words tumbled out.

'How did you cope after Dad left?'

Helen's gaze met hers. 'You find little things to get you through the day. Work, friends, a good book, keeping the house running.'

Sarah's grip tightened on her mug. 'But don't you get lonely?'

'Of course,' Helen admitted, 'but you can't let it consume you.'

A flicker of anger passed through Sarah. 'I hate that Dad just moved on like we meant nothing.'

Helen's sigh was almost inaudible. 'Life's messy, Sarah. People make mistakes, and sometimes there's no going back.'

The atmosphere grew tense when Sarah couldn't hold back her feelings any longer. 'I can't understand how you never say anything bad about Dad. After everything he did, how can you still defend him?'

Sarah leaned against the counter, her arms crossed as if to ward off the chill.

'You have a right to be angry. How can you not be angry?' Sarah's voice was a mix of bewilderment and a touch of resentment.

Helen was quiet for a moment, her fingers tracing the rim of her empty mug. 'Sarah, there's something I've never told you or anyone else,' she began, her voice low. 'It's a heavy secret, and I need you to promise me it stays between us. I've tried to tell you before, but I felt it wasn't the right time.

Now that you're an adult and you've had a serious relationship, I think you're better equipped to understand. I want you to see things from your dad's side too.'

A solemn nod from Sarah was her vow of silence.

Helen sighed, her eyes glistening with tears. 'I'm about to tell you something that won't be easy to process.'

Sarah nodded, a sense of foreboding settling in. 'I promise, I'll keep it a secret.'

Taking a deep breath, Helen began, 'Miguel is not your full brother. He's actually your half-brother.'

Sarah's eyes widened in shock. 'What? How is that possible?'

'When you were in grade school, your dad became so absorbed with his career that he hardly spent time with me, with us. He'd leave early, come home late, and even work weekends. Jorge became emotionally and physically distant from me; I was weak and . . . I turned to someone else. A single dad from your school. It was a brief escape from the loneliness, but I regretted it immediately,' Helen's words were barely a whisper, her eyes not leaving the tabletop.

Helen explained with a heavy heart, 'The damage was done. Jorge couldn't stay in the marriage after that, but he never denied Miguel and treated him as his own. He continued to support the family, even after my betrayal.'

Sarah felt her world tilt, a silent gasp escaped her lips, and a cold hand seemed to grip her heart. 'So, Dad left because . . .'

Helen's eyes finally met Sarah's, a silent stream of tears betraying her composed exterior. 'Yes. It was me. Your father couldn't live with me after that. Yet, he always provided for us, and kept my secret.'

Sarah's thoughts were a whirlwind. Her anger towards her father, once as solid as the ground beneath her feet, now felt like shifting sand. 'And he still helps us because . . .'

'Because he couldn't stay, but he also couldn't stop caring,' Helen finished for her, a look of pained admiration for the man she had wronged.

As the initial shock subsided, Sarah found herself in the unfamiliar territory of empathy towards the man she had refused to understand. Helen's secret didn't just change the narrative of their family's past, it challenged Sarah's own narrative of her break-up with Pete.

Sarah's world felt like it was falling apart. She'd always thought of her mom as a saint, and this revelation left her feeling betrayed. She wanted to be angry, but she loved her mom too much. She took a deep breath and tried to see it from her mom's perspective. She tried to understand the deep loneliness her mom had experienced in her marriage.

A tearful Sarah spoke softly, 'What happened to you and Miguel's father? Did he just leave too?'

'I was the one who broke things off with him. I knew what I had done was wrong.'

'Why didn't Dad stay when you broke things off with him?' Sarah asked.

'It was too late. Your dad couldn't bear to be with me. I tried, Sarah. I told him that I would change, but that wasn't enough for him.'

Sarah also tried to see it from her dad's point of view. She could understand why he had been harsh.

'Why didn't he give you chance . . . for the sake of our family?'

'I couldn't force him, Sarah.'

Sarah felt another tear escape, tracing a warm path down her cheek. 'Mom, I . . . I always thought of you as the wronged one. And now . . .' She choked on the words, her ideal image of her mother cracking before her eyes.

'I was the one who did wrong, anak,' Helen said, her voice tinged with regret. 'I'm a flawed human being. I made choices I'm not proud of. After your dad left, I did what I thought was necessary to survive, to keep us together.'

Sarah, although still in shock, found herself reassessing her mom. 'I need time to understand Dad. I'm still not ready to accept that he left us. I know his reason now. But how could he give up being with us? Maybe, one day, I'll talk to him again. But not now.'

'When you're ready, anak,' Helen replied. Her eyes were brimming with sorrow and fear as she observed her daughter grappling with the truth. 'I'm sorry, Sarah. I never meant to burden you with this. But I can't bear how resentful you are of your dad. I felt lonely in our marriage. Yes, he had a hand in that, but I didn't fix it. I want you to understand why I could never be angry with your dad.'

Sarah remembered Pete's parting words, about feeling trapped, needing space. It echoed too closely to her mother's own confession of loneliness. The parallel drew a line of pain straight through her heart. *Is that why Pete left? Because he felt alone, even with me?*

As they sat there, facing each other in the dimly lit kitchen, Sarah's mind was a whirlwind of emotions and questions, and she knew there was more to be said.

'Ma,' Sarah began tentatively, 'this is a lot to take in.'

Helen nodded, her gaze fixed on her daughter. 'I know, Sarah. I wanted to protect you from this truth for such a long time, but I also want you to understand why I couldn't speak ill of your father, no matter what happened between us.'

Sarah frowned, her thoughts still racing. 'I get that you had a tough time, but what about me? What about us, your kids? We never asked for any of this, and we're caught up in the consequences of your choices.'

Helen's eyes welled up with fresh tears. 'I'm so sorry, Sarah. You're right; you and Miguel didn't deserve any of this. I hope you can find it in your heart to forgive me someday.' Helen reached out, placing her hand over Sarah's. 'We all have our own battles, our own reasons. Sometimes they align with others, and sometimes they push us away.'

Sarah's anger began to soften as she saw the sincerity in her mother's eyes. She remembered the late nights her mother stayed up caring for her. 'I love you, Ma. I don't like what you did, but I still love you.'

Helen reached across the table, taking Sarah's hand in hers. 'Thank you, anak. That means everything to me.'

The air between them felt lighter as the burden of years lifted, replaced by an unspoken understanding and acceptance. They were both human, both searching for connection, for love, and both had found themselves lost along the way.

'Ma, I think I need a fresh start too. Marley invited me to Batlag Falls. It's just the break I need,' Sarah said, a hint of hope threading through her words.

'Sometimes, a little adventure can be a good thing. It's something your father and I lacked in our relationship, and I don't want you to make the same mistake.'

Sarah looked at her mom with a new-found determination. 'I'll take your advice, Ma. This trip to Batlag Falls is just what

I need. I'll find a way to break free from my routine and rediscover who I am.'

Helen smiled, a glimmer of hope in her eyes. 'I believe in you, Sarah. You're stronger than you think, just like your father always said.'

As they hugged each other goodnight, they knew they would both face the challenges of the coming day with courage and understanding. The secrets that had burdened them for so long were out in the open, and in their vulnerability, they found strength.

As Sarah climbed back into her bed, her mind was no longer a chaos of thoughts. Instead, she felt a sense of closure and the beginnings of a new journey. The darkness of the night had given way to the light of a new day, and Sarah was ready to embrace it with open arms.

Her room was filled with an unspoken promise of a new beginning, a tentative step towards healing old wounds.

Even though it had been difficult, Sarah felt that the conversation with her mom was a testament to their enduring bond. The night had been long, and the conversation longer, but she knew they had both found courage.

CHAPTER 9

Marley had briefed her ahead of time. The trip to Batlag Falls was going to be a prelude to the trip to Santa Ines. In her email, Marley had said: *Santa Ines is going to be physically exhausting, so I want you to have more time to prepare for that. I want your first adventure to be an uncomplicated nature trip.*

Sarah actually had butterflies in her stomach. She'd followed Marley's diet and exercise plan and she felt fitter than she did two weeks ago. This was it! Her first adventure. She commuted from Marikina to Eastwood Mall along C-5, their meet-up place. She had packed light: a backpack with her rash guard and board shorts (she was already wearing a swimsuit under her black T-shirt and khaki shorts), mosquito repellent, a snack composed of a chicken sandwich and a bottle of water, and a change of clothes. On the suggestion of Marley, she wore flip flops with ankle straps (other suggestions from Marley were outdoor sandals or aqua socks) because some parts of the falls were rocky. She had also put her phone into a clear ziplock sandwich bag.

When she got to the designated coffee shop, Marley was already there. She was wearing a tank top that showed off her toned and tanned arms, a bandana, rubber outdoor sandals, and cargo shorts.

'You're early!' Sarah said.

'Just wanted to be sure that I would already be here to welcome you to your adventure! Are you ready?'

'Never been more ready!'

'I'm parked at the basement. Let's go!'

Marley had a really cute lime-green compact car with a two-bike transport rack at the back. Sarah sighed. One day, she was going to have her own car just like Marley. She mentally reminded herself to ask Marley how she'd saved up for a car and if it was easy to learn how to drive.

'Dump your stuff on the back seat,' Marley instructed her. 'Have you had breakfast?'

'Yup, I made sure to get some before heading out.'

'Okay, good, that means we won't need to make too many stops. I'm planning to pass the Sierra Madre route so you can really enjoy the view.'

'You know what? I really haven't been out much. I live in Marikina, but I've never really been out of the Metro much. This is going to be my first time driving out to Sierra Madre.'

'Wow! You poor deprived girl. You are going to love the drive, I promise.'

They headed out to Marcos Highway. There was some weekday traffic but the road after Masinag Market was a lot less crowded. It was also entirely unfamiliar to Sarah. She was out in the sunlight on a weekday, and she was on a road that she had never encountered before. This was what she had been missing the whole time she was chasing the next step in her career ladder.

'This road gets us access to Sierra Madre. So, in two hours or less, you can actually get to the mountain. It's really the best view in the least amount of time, I think.'

'I didn't know it even existed.'

'There's a first for everything!'

Sarah's phone beeped: *How's the adventure going?* It was Benito.

Sarah replied: *What adventure?*

Benito: *Very funny, Sarah. Miguel told me. So, you can't lie yourself out of this one.*

Sarah: *Ugh. I'd better talk to Miguel. It's going very well! Did you know that you could get to the Sierra Madre from Eastwood City in two hours or less?*

Benito: *Yes. Why wasn't I invited?* 😔

Sarah: *I want this adventure (and Marley) all to myself.*

Benito: *Take me on the next one?*

Sarah: *I'll think about it. Stop bugging me already. I'll miss the view.*

'We can park on the side of the road when we get to higher altitude so you can take pictures,' Marley said.

'Thanks, Marley!'

Sarah watched the road clear up as they progressed. Thirty minutes into their trip, Sarah noticed fewer and fewer cars. Marley was right. The sight of mountains coming up in the horizon gave her the most wonderful feeling in the world. She felt free, like she had been cooped up in a cage and was finally out where she should be. At one point she felt her ears pop.

'That's the change in altitude kicking in,' Marley remarked.

Sarah looked to her right and saw the most fantastic panorama: rolling green hills and smoky blue and purple mountains as far as her eyes could see. It was Marley's cue to find a spot to park. They got down and just stared at what was in front of them. Both were quiet. Sarah couldn't find words for what she was feeling.

'It's beautiful, isn't it?' Marley asked.

Sarah felt tears burning her eyes. It was one of the most beautiful things she had seen. She had been to the beach with her mom and dad, but never to the mountains. Those were happier days then. She wondered what it would have been like if all of them had stayed together, if all of them had come here to see this spectacular view.

'Are you okay?' Marley asked when she didn't answer.

'I'm okay. I just haven't seen something like this before. It's overwhelming.'

'Do you want me to take your picture?'

'Yes, please.' She handed her phone to Marley after taking it out of the ziplock bag.

'I know it's corny but why don't we take a selfie shot together?' Sarah asked Marley. She just laughed and they both turned to the phone cam with their biggest smiles.

'We're not far,' Marley said. After a few more kilometres, she turned to the right where there was a sign that read: 'This way to Daranak Falls.'

'Batlag Falls is going to be farther along from Daranak Falls,' Marley explained. After they parked and got their bags out of the car, they walked down a bit and turned to a small hut where they paid the entrance fee. They had to cross a wooden bridge to get to Daranak. While crossing the bridge, Sarah saw a stream below where rocks were balanced on top of each other. They were all stable and yet they looked like they were precariously stacked.

'That's what they call rock balancing art,' Marley said.

'They're beautiful,' Sarah said.

'A couple of artists from the area started doing them after typhoon Ondoy to raise awareness about the importance of keeping the environment balanced.'

'Balancing rocks to show the natural balance in nature. That's really brilliant.'

'I know! And they really don't use any tools. They just use the natural weight of each rock to create equilibrium.'

They continued walking.

'Sarah, we'll pass by Daranak Falls first but we'll be spending more time at Batlag Falls.'

She followed Marley down a path, and she caught her breath when she saw the fourteen-metre waterfall cascading into a wide greenish-blue pool. She noticed that there were several teenagers already swimming in the pool.

'Wow!' was all Sarah could say.

'This waterfall can get pretty crowded, though. That's why I wanted to take you to Batlag. We can take pictures here later, on the way back.'

Sarah continued to follow Marely as the trail went uphill. She realized why a workout was part of Marley's adventure experience for her. Trekking was no joke. She found herself pausing in between the rocks fashioned into stairs to catch her breath. Marley was nice enough to notice her own pauses during the steep climb and slowed down her own pace to match Sarah's.

They finally reached a fence that announced their arrival at Batlag Falls. The fee was a bit steeper than Daranak. Also, they had to pay another fee to rent a table for their bags. She could see why there weren't as many people at Batlag Falls.

There was a whole wing of covered picnic tables where they paid their entrance fees, but they needed to go down another set of stairs to get to Batlag Falls. Sarah heard the inviting sound of the water as they went down the steps, though she couldn't help thinking of the upward climb that would wait for her.

She took in the view before proceeding to the falls. She felt she was in an enchanted space. It was much cooler at Batlag because trees were shading the entire area, making the water look greener. There was an island at the centre of the basin and on it was a stately balete tree that seemed to stand like a sentinel. The Batlag waterfall wasn't as high as Daranak but Sarah felt it was more beautiful because she could see it better up close. There was a rock on which anyone could easily perch and feel the power of the cascading water.

Marley and Sarah put their bags down and started putting on their rash guards and board shorts. There was no one else around.

'You know what, this is your day. Give me your phone. Head out into the water first and I'll take your pictures. Then, we can just enjoy the water after,' Marley said.

Sarah was so grateful. She left her beach towel on a flat rock and slowly edged into the water. Marley was so right in advising the slippers with straps because she could feel that the rocks underneath her feet were rough. The water was frightfully cold at first but after she dunked her whole body, including her head, into the water, her body adjusted to the temperature. Marley took a couple of shots of her floating in the pool at the base of the waterfall. Then Sarah climbed up the rock that she had seen earlier and sat down cross-legged. The water was falling over her back and shoulders and the noon sun was shining directly on her face. She closed her eyes. It was heaven. She felt like she could sit there forever, just listening to the sound of water falling and feeling the water wash over her. How could she have lived just going to and from the office or the mall for so long?

This was where she needed to be. She wanted more of this in her life.

'Hey, I think I have one hundred pictures of you already, forest goddess. I'm jumping in!' Marley called out to Sarah.

She saw Marley stow her phone inside a waterproof tote she left beside Sarah's bag. Marley whooped as she splashed into the pool. Sarah had never felt so carefree in her life. They spent a whole hour just swimming and getting their backs massaged by the waterfall.

Afterwards, they dried themselves at their picnic table and ate the lunch they had packed.

'It's so peaceful here,' Sarah said.

'That's why I love it,' Marley replied. 'I wish people would take care of places like this without having to make them private. Daranak is beautiful but it gets too crowded for my taste.'

'I'm in love with this waterfall,' Sarah said. Suddenly, she had an epiphany. A plan started to form in her head.

'Marley, I think I want to go on a waterfall adventure. I want to visit more of them. What do you think?'

'That's fantastic! This is your first. Well, technically, there are two waterfalls here so they can be your first and second. And then Santa Ines will be your third.'

'I'll count this as one. Santa Ines will be my second. Marley, I have some money saved. I want to visit more waterfalls across the country!'

'That's a true adventurer talking! I'll help you plan it!'

They sounded like two giddy schoolgirls talking about their crush. On the way back to Marley's car, Sarah spotted a small greenish-grey pebble and picked it up. *What did I learn from here?*

Later that night, Sarah opened up her digital journal and wrote:

If I start a blog, then this will be part of it.

Journal entry
First Stop: Batlag Falls

Hidden away from the urban sprawl, Batlag Falls felt like a realm suspended in time. The water here was an unusual shade of turquoise, almost ethereal in its beauty. As I stepped into the pool, I felt as if I was being baptized anew, free from the trappings of the modern world.

A small greenish-grey pebble.

A little extra effort and a little more patience spelled the difference between the crowd and some sacred space.

Act 2

The Destination

CHAPTER 10

'Anak, are you sure this is a good idea? I know you're hurting a lot right now but I'm not sure waterfall hopping is the solution. I was okay with Batlag Falls since it's near, but I'm not sure about you going to different provinces,' Sarah's mom said. Her brows were knitted together in her signature look of worry.

'Ma, it might sound like a whim but it's not. I'm really serious about this.'

Sarah had just explained to her mom her plan: First, she was going to Santa Ines Falls with Marley. Then, she was planning a grand tour of five more waterfalls, crossing to the Visayas via a plane ride to Cebu (there was an upcoming seat sale offered by a local airline, so she was planning to grab that in a few days) where she was going to visit Kawasan Falls. Then, she was going to take a boat ride to Bohol to hunt down Mag-aso (Twin) Falls. From Bohol, she planned to take a fastcraft to Siquijor to visit Cambugahay Falls. After Siquijor, she planned to go back to Bohol and take a boat to Cagayan de Oro. It was going to be the jump-off point for a land trip to Iligan City to visit the very alluring Tinago Falls, and then finally she wanted to head out to South Cotabato to visit Lake Sebu and the famed Seven Falls (literally, seven waterfalls that could be visited through a rigorous hike or be seen from an exciting zip-line ride).

Ever since Batlag Falls, Sarah and Marley couldn't stop talking about the next leg of Sarah's waterfall adventure. When they had headed back to the city, they had stopped by at a bookstore to buy a map of the Philippines and then sat down at a café to talk strategy. Sarah had never been more excited about a project. Sure she'd had project management challenges all throughout her two-year BPO career but it had never felt this important. This was the adventure of *her life*.

'Is this going to be safe?' her mom asked one more time, just when the doorbell rang.

Sarah headed to the door. She knew it was going to be Anya and Benito because she had invited them over to discuss her plan too. Sarah hugged them both when she saw them.

'Hi, Tita Helen!' Anya called out to Sarah's mom. She kissed her on the cheek.

'Tita Helen, you look better and better every time I see you!' Benito teased.

It was true, though. Helen Silvestre was a beautiful woman who had maintained her figure even after raising two kids by herself. Sarah often wondered why her mom never remarried. She saw guys, whether her mom's age or younger, actually checking out her mom. She was *that* attractive. But now, Sarah knew better. Her mom must have been plagued with feelings of guilt for so long. Having another relationship must have been the last thing on her mind.

'Benito, you know I love you! Do you want some cookies?' Sarah's mom said as she headed out to the kitchen.

'Do you even need to ask?' Benito said as he trailed after Sarah's mom. Her mom made killer cookies too, just the right combination of chewy and crunchy. And she didn't stint on the ingredients.

Sarah, Benito, and Anya sat around the glass table in the sala as they discussed Sarah's plan. Sarah's mom left them to talk, leaving a big pitcher of iced tea and a plate of her famous cookies on the table.

'You know I'm all for it, Sarah,' Anya began, 'but I'm worried that this is all so sudden. This is the first time you'll be travelling. And you'll be travelling alone!'

'I agree with Anya,' Benito said.

How could she explain to them how important this was?

'I know this sounds crazy but, guys, you know I've never really done anything for myself like this. Now that I have the funds, I think I shouldn't miss out on this. The stars have aligned! I mean what were the chances of a seat sale opening up just when I was thinking of flying to Cebu? It's a sign from the universe!'

'Sarah, I totally support you,' Anya replied, 'but can you skip Mindanao?'

'No. It's part of my plan.'

'What did your mom say?' Benito asked.

'She's just as worried as you guys. Maybe even more worried, actually. But I am twenty-four! For goodness' sake, I don't need my mother's permission!'

'We're just looking out for you,' Anya said.

'Why don't I just go with you, Sarah?' Benito suggested, a concerned look in his eyes.

'What? No!' Sarah did not see that coming.

'You know, that sounds like a good idea,' Anya said. 'If I didn't already have a big project at the agency, I would go with you too. How awesome would that be? It would be the first time we'd be travelling as a barkada!' Anya sounded excited. 'Except I really can't go,' Anya said. 'So, I hereby appoint Benito as my official representative. What do you say, Benito?'

'No!' Sarah almost shouted. 'Guys, this is my journey of self-discovery!'

'I can free myself up,' Benito said, as if he didn't hear what Sarah said.

'Exactly,' Anya said, also ignoring Sarah, 'being the child of owner has a lot of benefits like emergency friend protection.' His family's business had grown in the past decade, and they had moved from Marikina to an exclusive subdivision in Quezon City when Benito was in his senior year of high school.

'Sarah, I have relatives in Visayas and Mindanao from my mom's side. I think that would really come in handy when you go down south,' Benito said.

'I'm sorry, but no. No one is going with me,' Sarah said. She hoped they heard her tone of finality.

She saw Anya and Benito exchange a look.

'Fine,' Anya said, 'but you had better update us on your whereabouts every step of your way.'

'Okay,' Sarah said.

'Promise us, Sarah,' Benito said.

'Promise.'

'What about your job hunt?' Anya asked.

'It's temporarily on hold,' Sarah answered. That was one of the things that made her feel guilty, especially with her mom. Her plan had been to take over her dad when it came to paying for Miguel's tuition. When she got retrenched, that plan got derailed.

'Where exactly are you going, Sarah?' Benito asked, 'My mom's family is from the south. I can make calls if you need a place to stay.'

Sarah silently admitted to herself that Benito's offer sounded very tempting.

'Wait, let me get my map,' Sarah said. She ran to her room and came back with a national map.

'I'm going to Cebu first,' she said, pointing to the narrow island smack in the middle of Visayas, between Bacolod and Bohol. I'm planning to visit Kawasan Falls in Badian, Cebu, first. After visiting Kawasan, I'm planning to take a boat to Bohol where I'm going to visit Mag-aso Falls.'

'What? That's all you're going to see in Cebu?' Benito asked. 'I mean, this is your first time going to Cebu and you're planning to miss the whole city? You won't even pass by Lapu-Lapu? I think you should think this plan through some more.'

Sarah was irritated with Benito's tone. Among the three of them, it was Benito who was the most well travelled. Instead of giving her helpful tips, he was making her sound like an idiot.

'I know there's a lot to see in Cebu, Benito. But I have to focus on what I want to accomplish. I'm after the waterfalls. That's it. This won't be my last adventure. I'll make sure to put other stuff in the itinerary when my goal is to explore Cebu.'

'Okay, okay. Calm down. Wow. So, you're going to be taking a three-hour bus ride all the way to the mountains on the southern side of Cebu, which is where Badian is, near

Moalboal; then you'll be riding back to the city, another three hours, to take a ferry. I suggest you stay overnight so you don't get tired out. That way, you may want to visit Moalboal before heading back to the city. I mean, it's Moalboal that's usually the destination and Badian is the side trip. But with you, it's the opposite! There are easier itineraries, you know,' Benito said.

Sarah was still annoyed with Benito. Why couldn't he see it from her point of view? This wasn't a typical island tour for her. 'I'm not thinking of what's easier, Benito.' *But should I?* She wouldn't have known these things on her own. Even Marley, whom she considered the expert when it came to adventure, admitted that it had been a while since she visited Cebu and Bohol.

'Okay, what's next?'

'I'm going to visit Mag-aso Falls while I'm in Bohol. Then I'll take a ferry to Siquijor to visit Cambugahay Falls. After that, I'll go back to Bohol so I can take a boat ride to Cagayan de Oro.'

'You do realize that the ferry ride from Bohol to Siquijor is two hours, right?'

'No. But I don't mind.'

'Okay. What are your plans in Cagayan de Oro?'

'It's just a stop, actually. I want to proceed to Iligan from there.'

'Iligan? Are you serious?'

'Why? That's where Tinago Falls is.'

'I advise against it, Sarah. I'm serious.'

Benito did look serious. His usually carefree demeanour had changed to one of concern. His thick brows were meeting together. And his broad shoulders were hunched. Sarah could feel the tension.

'Thanks for your opinion, Benito, but it's still in my itinerary.'

'Sarah, why do you have to be so—'

'What, Benito?'

'Stubborn!'

Stubborn Sarah. That was new. 'So, Benito, which boat or ferry services should I take coming from Cebu?' Sarah asked. She wanted to distract him.

Benito stretched and put his game face on. 'There are three fast ferry providers to Tagbilaran. I would go with the one with more trips; that way, you get a more flexible schedule.'

Anya laughed, 'So, you still think taking Benito along isn't a good idea?'

'He's definitely my travel consultant now!' Sarah laughed along.

Honestly, Benito was the perfect travel companion. He was never boring. And lately, ever since he'd broken up with his girlfriend, Gia, he was looking cuter and fitter. To be honest, he was hot. But it was weird to think of Benito as hot. Sarah tried to erase those last three observations from her mind. But it was too late.

CHAPTER 11

Sarah took a good two weeks to prepare for Santa Ines. Marley clarified that the name of the waterfall they were visiting was Kinabuan Falls. In fact, the more hardcore destination in Tanay, Rizal, would be Mt Irid. But Marley told her that Kinabuan Falls was hard enough, and it really wasn't for newbies. She followed Marley's simple fitness plan, which was focused on a combination of aerobic and anaerobic training with some stretching and balancing exercises. She had to be physically fit, otherwise it was going to be hard for her to catch up with the group. Miguel also had to train her in mountain biking: climbing uphill on low gear, negotiating rough paths, and riding over rocky terrain. She and Miguel had fun looking around their village for practice terrain.

'I envy you, Ate,' Miguel confessed. 'I've always wanted to go on that river trail. But be careful, okay?'

'You sound like my kuya now,' Sarah said, smiling.

'Okay, one more uphill climb.'

'Ugh! It's torture!' Sarah said, mopping her brow with a knit fabric towel.

'C'mon! This is the hard part but you're going to love the destination.'

'I'm hooked, Miguel. I promise to get my own mountain bike and helmet soon.'

'I'm just happy that you're getting to appreciate one of the things I love.'

'Thanks for helping me, bro.'

'Anytime, sis! Are you ready for your waterfall trip down south?'

'I don't know if I'm one hundred per cent ready. But Marley and Benito have really been a big help.'

'You're my idol, Ate!'

On the day of the river trail ride, Marley had to pick up Sarah from her house because of her bike gear. She reached Sarah's house at around 7.00 a.m. Together, they mounted Miguel's bike onto the second bike rack of her car. Marley explained that they would be driving through Marcos Highway again, then onto Marilaque Highway. Sarah and Marley were dressed in trek gear: swimsuits, cycling shorts under board shorts, running shoes, and dri-fit jerseys on top. Marley definitely got away with a sleeveless jersey. They also carried backpacks. At Marley's suggestion, Sarah kept her backpack light: lightweight knit fabric towel, rash guard, sandwich lunch, two bananas for snacks, one litre of water, and a flashlight.

The meet-up point was at the main highway, after Cabading. Marley pulled over onto the verge and they waited for the rest of the river trail team to show up. There were going to be five of them. Joel, who was a friend of Marley's from college, soon arrived. He brought along his brother,

Eric, and Eric's girlfriend, Ana. Apparently, they'd done the trail before, but they wanted to make better time than the last trip because they had ended up heading home in pitch dark. They wanted to move faster on this trip so they could get home by sunset at least. They took a risk, taking in a newbie like Sarah, but Marley reassured the rest of the team that Sarah had been busy preparing for the river trail ride for the last two weeks.

After the initial greetings, they were all business. Marley took their bikes off the car, and next thing Sarah knew, they were all headed downhill for the next fifteen minutes. She and Miguel had practised downhill riding several times. At first, she'd been scared by how fast she was going but with proper use of the brakes, she had actually enjoyed downhill rides. The descent from the main highway was exhilarating for Sarah but it also made her think of the ascent on their return trip. It was going to be tough!

The river trail itself was an amazing experience for Sarah. Despite some difficulty navigating rocks while crossing streams and rivers, Sarah had never experienced so much natural beauty in her life: a view of mountains and forests in all directions, the clear water of the streams and rivers they were crossing (she was tempted to just jump in but she knew there was a reward waiting for them in Kinabuan Falls), and the canopy of a clear blue sky above them. It was hot but she felt refreshed by the splashes from the streams and rivers. Marley also reminded her to take a sip of water whenever she could to avoid cramps from dehydration.

At their eighth river crossing, they saw small cottages made of cogon and bamboo. 'We're in the Dumagat territory,' Joel announced to their group. Marley had already briefed Sarah about the indigenous tribe that lived near the waterfalls. There was a steel arch that announced they were in Barangay Santa Ines. They all headed to the barangay hall where they had to register. They also left some canned goods and fruits as gift for the Dumagat chieftain (it was customary and good manners, according to Marley). The Dumagats were an indigenous community in Rizal Province. They were the original forest inhabitants and had close ties with the land. Even though local lawmakers didn't consider them important enough for decision-making, Marley explained that it was important for trekkers to pay their respects to the tribe. The group left their bikes chained to posts at the multipurpose hall of the Dumagats and proceeded on foot from there.

'Eleven more river crossings to go!' Eric said cheerily after they left the barangay hall. By their eleventh river crossing, they actually had to form a line in the water that was up to their thighs (according to Joel, the water could reach their waists if it were the rainy season) and half-swim to the other side. Marley had already warned her about the limatiks (or river leeches). It was a good thing Sarah wasn't the type to faint at the sight of blood. She got one on her leg and it was pretty disgusting to remove it, though it didn't hurt at all.

When they finally reached Kinabuan Falls, Sarah marvelled at the serene sight. It was enchanting. The waterfall and pool were hidden under a thick cover of trees that were filtering out the afternoon sun. From afar, the water looked bluish green. Closer up, it was so clear that she could see the mossy rocks beneath the water. Sarah felt peaceful just looking at the water.

They all first sat down to eat their packed lunches. Both Joel and Marley were very strict about not leaving any trash around and they all kept their used plastic bags and napkins in their backpacks.

After lunch, Marley, Sarah, and Ana put on their rash guards and headed over to the water. The guys were busy with their DSLRs. After a rigorous workout in the sun, the cold water was a welcome treat for Sarah.

'Good for you,' Ana said to Sarah after Marley explained to her about Sarah's waterfall plan.

'My mom and my best friends aren't thrilled, though. They think I'm being careless because I want to go alone. They don't understand that it's really important to me.'

'It's only natural that the people who care about you want to protect you, Sarah,' Marley said.

'How did you convince your own parents and friends?' Sarah asked Marley.

'I did my share of compromise. I made sure to update my parents every step of the way. They eventually got used to my style. But I did it one step at a time.'

'Do you think I'm rushing it by going to several destinations?'

'Each adventurer is unique. You're here, now, because you're preparing for something bigger. I agree that you shouldn't take on more than you can handle. But, I've found that a little stretch is also good.'

'That's true, Marley,' Ana agreed, 'I never went on an adventure before I met Eric. I didn't even know how to bike!'

'Really?' Sarah marvelled over Ana's statement. Ana was such a natural on her mountain bike.

'Yeah!' Ana said, laughing, 'Would you believe that? But Eric was really patient with me. And now look where I am today! I'm really happy that I pushed myself.'

Sarah thought about what Marley and Ana just shared. She still had a lot to learn but she felt really inspired.

They all stayed at the waterfall for another hour, and then started heading back. Sarah picked up a pebble from the side of the basin. This time, it was sand-coloured with layers of white. They made good time on the return hike to the Dumagat village. Sarah trailed behind, but Marley made sure to keep to the back. That's what trek leaders did. She encouraged Sarah and made sure she stayed hydrated. Because they all knew the terrain from that morning, they got back to the Marilaque Highway just in time for sunset. It was a good thing that they still had some daylight because Sarah had to dismount from her bike three to four times. She was extremely embarrassed. There was a moment when she panicked because her legs got wobbly with fatigue. Marley helped her raise her seat to avoid knee pain and told her to take a food break to keep up her energy. But, in the end, she told Sarah it was better to dismount rather than push uphill when she felt unsteady.

'I'm sorry, Marley,' Sarah said, 'I should have practised more.'

'Uphill is really tough. But you did well enough on the trek. It's a good thing we still have a lot of light.'

Despite the delay, everyone cheered Sarah on. When they finally reached the highway, they all congratulated her for completing her first-ever river trail.

'Guys, I'm so sorry for holding us up,' Sarah said to the trek team.

'Hey,' Eric replied, 'It's okay. There's no shame in walking up a hill.'

'Yeah,' Marley replied, patting Sarah on the back. 'There's a first time for everything. And you did it! You finished your first river trail. I'm so proud of you, Sarah.'

Despite the exhaustion, the sweat dripping down her heated face, Sarah felt a deep sense of accomplishment. What Marley said made her glow inside. She *did* feel proud of herself. It was different, incomparable to how she felt about meeting quotas at work. She touched the pebble in her pocket.

Journal entry
Second Stop: Kinabuan Falls

A treasure tucked away in the mountains of Santa Ines, Tanay, Rizal, Kinabuan Falls was a sanctuary of natural beauty. It was more than just a scenic spot, it was a place of spiritual healing for me. The local indigenous community manages the falls. I learned a lot here.

Sand-coloured stone with layers of white.

Persistence has its rewards.

CHAPTER 12

Sarah took a deep breath. It had taken her a month to plan and book her tickets and accommodations. And now, here she was at NAIA Terminal 3 two hours before her estimated time of departure, but her flight was delayed by an hour. Sarah was a little jittery because every hour counted in her itinerary. She had to check in at the hotel in the city first and then take a bus from the Cebu South Bus Terminal. The trip from the bus terminal to Badian was going to take at least two hours. While she waited, she played back the conversation she had with Benito on the way to the airport.

'I'm going to miss you,' Benito said.

'It's not like I'm going to be gone for a month, Benito.'

'I really don't understand why I just couldn't go with you. You'll get so many benefits.'

'Like what?'

'Like free accommodations at my relatives' digs.'

Sarah had to admit that it would have really helped. She had the money, yes, but she still wanted to save as much as she could. It was just her pride holding up her decision to go alone. *And* so much had changed.

Usually, Benito always paid attention to the girlfriend of the moment. She and Anya were used to it. That was just Benito. But then, lately, it was weird that he didn't have anyone in tow. Ever since her break-up with Pete, Benito had *always* been around. He hung out with Miguel. He offered to drive her anywhere at the most random hours. It was *nice*. But she was scared too. *Did it mean anything?* She didn't want to make it mean anything.

But she also caught herself thinking: *What if we were together?* Because, frankly, being single, all of a sudden, gave her a weird filter when it came to Benito. She realized that, except for his grade school years, he'd always been with someone. It was the same for her too. Six years was a long time. She'd gotten used to having Pete by her side. She never really looked around.

Seeing Benito as a possibility made her head spin. She didn't want to assume. She didn't want to change anything about their friendship. But she just couldn't stop thinking about it. *What's wrong with me?*

When she dug deep enough, she realized that she didn't want Benito to come along because she was scared: scared of being alone with him, scared that their friendship would get weird. She couldn't tell him all this, though, so she convinced herself that it was her pride.

When they got to the airport, he helped her with her backpack and carry-on luggage. Sarah wanted to travel light, but she decided to take along her laptop. They stood awkwardly in front of the car for a few seconds.

'Take care of yourself, Steady Sarah,' he said, and reached out to hug her.

She smelled his crisp, clean cologne. She could feel his muscles through his shirt. *Focus, Sarah, focus.* She looked up at him and found him smiling. How come she never noticed how disarming his smile was?

'I'm just a phone call away, okay?' He reminded her.
She nodded and watched him go back into his car.

First flight ever, she wrote in her journal. She had decided
to take a travel journal along with her. She didn't want to
miss any details. She made sure to get a window seat. When
the pilot announced that they were taking off, Sarah felt
butterflies in her stomach. *This is it.* She watched the roads,
trees, and houses below her shrink, until Manila looked like a
landscape for ants.

It was an uneventful hour-long flight. Beside her was a
businessman who dozed off as soon as the plane took off.
She read the in-flight magazine for a few minutes and then
decided that she should take a nap too. When she woke up,
she realized she had missed the in-flight snack trolley, and
they were about to land at the Mactan Cebu International
Airport. Sarah quickly blotted her face and fixed her ponytail.

'Cebu South Terminal, po,' she said to the airport taxi driver.
'You're from Manila?' the driver asked.
'Yes, Kuya,' she said. The driver laughed, 'It's manong
here in Bisaya,' he said, still smiling. Sarah could tell that he
was just being helpful.
'Sorry po, Manong,' she said. It took them under an hour
to get to the bus terminal.

After paying her fare, Sarah took out her printed-out notes and headed towards the ticketing counter. She was surprised at how organized the bus terminal was. She chose one of the three bus lines plying the route to Badian (and Moalboal) and was surprised that the waiting area was air-conditioned, as if she was at an airport terminal. By then, Sarah's stomach was rumbling. It was a good thing that there were snack bars around the terminal, and she got herself a sandwich and some juice. It wasn't long before the bus heading out to Badian was announced on the PA system. As soon as she boarded the bus, she told the conductor her plan to get to Kawasan Falls. The conductor told her she could get off at the Matutinao Church. The bus ride was going to take two hours, so Sarah took the opportunity to doze off again.

After a good thirty-minute nap, Sarah woke up to stunning views on the way to Badian. They made several stops, and she made sure to try the Carcar chicharron. She bought lechon for her lunch at the falls and paired it off with pusô, or rice cooked in coconut leaves. She also tried some bibingka from Mantalungon. The bibingka was different from what she was used to in Manila: it was a simple white no-frills rice cake that had a toasted top. It was still warm when she bit into it. It was so good that she closed her eyes just to savour it.

After another hour, the bus conductor approached her. 'Miss, this is your stop,' he said. When she got off, she just asked around and was directed to a trail leading to Kawasan Falls. She joined several other small groups who were heading the same way. It was a weekday, so she was sure there won't be too many people at the falls. It took twenty minutes for them to reach their destination.

The path itself was easy (compared to her river crossing expedition with Marley). It was a pleasant walk even with her carry-on luggage. She could hear the waterfall in the distance and birds singing. Kawasan Falls were made up of three waterfalls, but she planned to just enjoy herself at the first level. The first waterfall was a sight to behold. It gushed from a rock covered with foliage, forty metres above the basin of clear bluish-green water.

Sarah rented a table and sat down for a very pleasant picnic of lechon, pusô, and Coke from a nearby kiosk, as she watched the hypnotic waterfall. After eating lunch, Sarah rested a bit and then took a dip in the freshwater pool. She felt silly renting a bamboo raft all to herself, but it was definitely worth it as she floated towards the falls and experienced a wonderful back massage from the pressure of the falling water. She enjoyed the rest of the afternoon just swimming and lounging. She made sure to pick up another small pebble. She was getting the hang of it. This was her third one. It was smooth and bluish black. *What did I learn from here?* Doing things alone was nothing to be scared about; it was a joy, in fact.

Before leaving the falls, she bought fresh buko from a vendor. She had the top lopped off and sipped the fresh, naturally sweet juice straight from the shell. After that, she had the buko cut into two and ate scoops of the gelatinous flesh using a coconut scraper.

Following Benito's advice, she didn't stay until evening but proceeded via bus to Moalboal where she stayed overnight at a little family-run resort. The next day, she joined a tourist group going to the Tuble Marine Sanctuary where she spent the morning snorkelling in shallow water rich with corals and marine life.

As Sarah gently glided through the crystal-clear waters of the Tuble Marine Sanctuary, her eyes were immediately captivated by the vibrant underwater tapestry below. The surface of the water acted like a lens, magnifying the riot of colours and activity in the shallow reef. It felt like entering a different world, a world where time slowed down, and every breath was a gateway to new wonders.

The coral gardens were a masterpiece of nature's artistry. They sprawled beneath her like a living mosaic, with corals of every shape and hue. Branching corals reached out towards the light, their intricate structures a playground for small, vividly coloured fish. Soft corals swayed gently in the current, their surfaces dotted with tiny, star-like polyps.

Schools of fish in dazzling patterns and colours darted in and out of the coral crevices. Clownfish, bold in their orange and white stripes, played hide and seek among the anemones, while parrotfish, dressed in their best blues and greens, nibbled on the coral.

The sanctuary was alive with movement. Sarah could see starfish slowly making their way across the sandy floor, their colours a stark contrast against the white sand. She was in awe as she saw some sea turtles, a rare sight, graceful and serene, glide past her, their flippers moving with a gentle rhythm.

The sunlight, filtering through the water, created a dance of light and shadow, adding a magical quality to the scene.

As she floated, suspended in this aquatic paradise, Sarah felt a profound sense of connection and peace. The marine sanctuary was more than just a beautiful place; Sarah knew that she was witnessing something truly special, a moment that would stay with her long after she returned to the surface.

I've finally done it. Sarah triumphantly sent out a group update of her first leg via group chat to her mom, Miguel, Marley, Anya . . . and Benito.

As she checked her phone, she noticed that she'd missed a call from an unknown number. *Sorry, I missed your call. Please let me know what this is about and I'll get back to you*, she texted back. She wondered who it was from and what it was about. *If it's important, they'll get back to me.*

Journal entry
Third Stop: Kawasan Falls

Located in the beautiful province of Cebu, Kawasan Falls offered more than just a stunning view. The rushing waters had carved intricate patterns into the limestone, creating natural artwork that left me awestruck. To say I was mesmerized would be an understatement.

Small, smooth, bluish-black stone.

Doing things alone was nothing to be scared about; it was a joy, in fact.

CHAPTER 13

Sarah took Benito's advice and got a ticket for the fast ferry with the most number of trips from Cebu to Tagbilaran, Bohol. She went for the afternoon trip since she had spent the morning snorkelling and travelling back to the city.

The ferry ride took two hours but that was enough to nauseate her. She just wanted to be on land already. As soon as she got off at Tagbilaran, she immediately took a taxi to Antequera. It took her an hour to reach her hotel there. After she had checked in and deposited her things at the hotel, she made plans to get to Mag-aso Falls.

It was Sarah's first time riding a habal-habal, which she took to get to Mag-aso Falls. It was uneventful, though, just like riding a tricycle. She did get a little worried when the driver took on more passengers on the way to Barangay Can-omay. She got the driver's cell phone number so she could let him know when to pick her up again from her swim at Mag-aso Falls.

It was intriguing to get to the falls because the stone path that led downwards cut through a lush forest. She took out her mosquito repellent, silently congratulating herself on being such a girl scout, and slathered the lotion generously on her arms and legs. An abundance of trees surrounded the waterfall and the basin. The websites and travel blogs had pointed out that the stone stairs had 197 steps. While it was easy going down, Sarah already anticipated the cardio workout going up and was reminded of her uphill ride from Kinabuan Falls.

After paying several entrance fees, she finally got to see the beautiful twin falls (slightly marred by the earthquake that hit Bohol in 2013 but, otherwise, still a sight to behold). The two cascades fell from a height of 25 feet into the deep catch basin. Sarah made sure to take a souvenir selfie at the viewing deck. A little touristy, but who cared? It was her first time in Bohol, and this was her fourth waterfall. She rented a little table for her backpack and snacks, which she had bought before the descent because there were no stores near the waterfalls, took off her T-shirt, and put on her trusty rash guard. She headed into the water. By now, she knew how cold waterfalls usually were, so she entered the water gradually. There was hardly anyone at the falls. She felt lucky that she had the place practically all to herself.

While it really wasn't sunny in the area, Sarah noticed the sky darken after an hour of idyllic swimming in the basin. She was in a makeshift salbabida floater made out of the rubber tubing of a tire when the first drops of rain fell. Something told her this was not a good sign. She started paddling herself towards the shallow end of the basin. She could have gone in the other direction, but she felt that higher ground, near the falls, was too slippery to reach. In just a matter of seconds, the basin water started rising as the rain fell harder. Sarah was flailing in the water, unable to get her bearings. The current was so strong, she felt herself getting pulled into it. She grabbed onto whatever rocks were protruding on the shoal. She didn't care that she'd hurt her arm in the process. She pulled herself out, but barely. In her panic to get out of the water, Sarah slipped on a rock and ended up injuring her ankle. One of the caretakers at the falls saw her and was quick to help her up to dry land.

In horror, Sarah watched as the water rose higher, turning a muddy brown as it crashed downriver. It was just a matter of seconds. She could have still been in the water. Sarah shuddered in the rain.

'Makatindog ka, Miss?' the caretaker asked her. She looked up at him and replied, 'Sorry po, hindi po ako makaintindi.' She felt ashamed that she didn't understand him. She should have tried to learn some basic Bisaya before heading down south.

'Can you stand?' the caretaker asked again, this time in Tagalog. She tried to stand by herself. She felt a shooting pain in her right leg. She looked down and saw blood flowing down the lower side of her leg. *Not good.* She shook her head.

'I'll call some other people to help you up the steps.' *The 197 steps!* She dreaded the ascent. As she sat waiting for the caretaker to come back with companions, she reached around her and picked up a sharp little pebble, it was grey with streaks of white, its edges slightly serrated. She let the edges of the stone bite into her palm. *What did I learn from here?* Honestly, she felt stupid. She should have checked the weather forecast beforehand. She should have learned a little Bisaya. She should have been more careful. Badly bruised and wounded, Sarah still counted herself lucky.

When the two men helped her up, she realized that she could still hobble despite the pain. She called the habal-habal driver who had taken her to the falls to let him know that she was on her way up. The caretaker helped her retrieve her backpack, and then he and another companion helped her make the tortuous uphill climb.

Sarah was so grateful to the two men that she gave them each a tip for helping her reach the top of the stairs. The habal-habal driver also took extra care to help her mount the wooden board that extended from the driver's seat. The trip back to the town proper wasn't so bad. She got a lot of help from fellow passengers as she rode a jeepney back to Tagbilaran. Her plan had been to go to Panglao Island from Mag-aso, but that had to take a backseat. She took a taxi back to her hotel in Antequera.

She dreaded hearing the words 'I told you so', but she had promised her family and friends that she would let them know what was going on with her trip every step of the way. She thought of whom to call first without sounding an alarm. She decided on Anya. She was generally level-headed. Sarah was sure Anya wouldn't panic.

'Omigod, Sarah!' Anya screamed from the other end of the phone. Okay, not a good call. Maybe she should have phoned Benito instead. 'I told you to take Benito with you!' And there it was, the dreaded 'I told you so'.

'I'm calling Benito right now!'

'Would you please stop shouting into my ear?' Sarah requested. 'It's just an ankle injury. No bones or tendons were affected. I'll be fine in a day, I think.'

'So, you're still planning to go on with your trip?' Anya asked. She wasn't shrieking any more but she was making her displeasure clear to Sarah.

'Yes.'

'Ugh! I'm calling Benito right now.'

'Relax. I'll call him myself.'

'No, you call your mother right now. And tell her that Benito is going to follow you to Bohol.'

'No way!'

'I bet you haven't called Tita Helen.'

'I haven't.'

'See? Make sure to call her. I'll ask Benito to call you after I talk to him.'

'Sarah?' She could feel Benito's concern over the phone.

'Hi, Benito.'

'Tell me where you're staying. I'm taking the first flight out to Bohol.'

'You don't have to. I don't want to impose.'

'You're injured. Either you go home right now after taking a rest or I go with you on the rest of your trip. Choose.'

'Benito . . .' Sarah hated how whiny she sounded. But she really didn't want to complicate things.

'You know that I'm doing this because I care about you, right?'

'I know. It's just that, I feel ashamed. You're going to spend unnecessarily just because of me.'

'Helping out a friend is *not* an unnecessary expense.'

'But what about your work?'

'I'll think of something. My dad won't mind. Besides, I haven't been on a break in a year. But, Sarah . . .' Benito trailed off.

'What?'

'I won't force it. If you really don't want me to come over, I won't bulldoze my way.'

Sarah knew it was her chance to say no with finality. All of a sudden, the pain she was feeling in her leg made her feel vulnerable. What was so wrong with having one of her best friends help her out? At the back of her mind, there was still that niggling 'what if' about Benito. Maybe it was time to find out?

'Okay.'

'That's all I need, Sarah. I'm taking the first flight out to Tagbilaran tomorrow.'

'Thanks, Benito. I owe you.'

'Big time.'

Sarah told him where she was staying. After she put down the phone, she actually felt relieved. *This was it. There was no turning back.*

Journal entry
Fourth Stop: Mag-aso Falls

Mag-aso was like a hidden gem. The descent to the falls was a steep trail that wound through the forest, but the sweat and effort were well worth it. The towering cliffs surrounding the falls created a secluded paradise, ideal for introspection or a peaceful getaway. I got into a little accident here, so this was one of the most unforgettable waterfalls I've ever encountered. I'll talk more about safety precautions during waterfall adventures. That's a whole other entry to look forward to.

Little, sharp, grey stone with streaks of white and with slightly serrated edges.

Being adventurous isn't the same as being foolhardy.

CHAPTER 14

Sarah sat on the hotel bed, her leg elevated on a pile of cushions. The bandage around her ankle felt like a straitjacket, but it was necessary after what had happened at Mag-aso Falls. Apart from that, she had a cold compress on her ankle as advised by the doctor at the hotel clinic. She winced as she shifted her weight, memories of her accident flooding back—the rush of the water, the slip of her foot, the cold, gut-wrenching fear as she realized she could actually get seriously hurt.

Her phone buzzed on the nightstand. It was a message from Benito: *Booked a ticket already. Don't worry, I'll be there soon.*

Sarah felt a pang of both relief and uncertainty. Benito was coming, but what did that mean for her? *We'll need to share hotel accommodations. Can I handle that kind of closeness right now?* she wondered, then pushed the thought away. *I'll cross that bridge when I get there.*

Sarah lay back against the pillows. The painkillers were beginning to take the edge off the throbbing in her ankle, but nothing seemed to numb a sudden surge of memories. It was in moments like these—vulnerable, hurt, alone—that she missed Pete the most.

Predictable Pete, her friends called him, and it was meant endearingly. He was the guy who always remembered to check the car's oil level, the one who would text her if there was a storm warning, the person who had a tool for every job tucked away in his meticulously organized garage. Pete had been a constant, a safe harbour in every unpredictable storm. Until he wasn't.

Her eyes darted back to her phone. One call could provide the emotional support she was craving. But it wasn't Benito she was thinking of; it was Pete, her Predictable Pete.

Her thoughts slid into a reverie, a doorway to a different time.

Two years ago

The air was brisk, filled with the scent of rain on concrete. Sarah had been standing outside the mall, cursing herself for leaving her umbrella behind. The downpour had started just as she had finished her shopping, and there she was, trapped and drenched. Her phone buzzed.

'Look across the street, Sarah,' Pete's voice came through, a hint of laughter in his tone.

There, across the swirling river of rainwater and hurried pedestrians, was Pete, under the wide expanse of a blue-and-white-striped umbrella. She sprinted across at the break in traffic, laughing as she ducked beside him, shaking like a wet puppy.

'You always think of everything,' she said, her eyes bright with unshed rain or unspoken words.

'I just don't want you catching a cold, that's all,' Pete replied, his voice as warm as the arm he wrapped around her shoulders.

As they walked, the rhythm of their steps was matched by the easy cadence of their conversation. Sarah talked about her day, her meetings, her officemates who made her laugh. Pete listened, interjecting his thoughts and pragmatic views.

'Aren't you glad I caught you before you crossed the street?' he chuckled, squeezing her a little closer to his side.

'My umbrella is safe and sound . . . in the office,' she said, jokingly. She was still silently chiding herself for forgetting her umbrella.

'Don't worry about it. I'm here now.'

Sarah smiled and looped her arm in his as the rain fell all around them.

Later that night, Sarah sat hunched over her laptop, her fingers tirelessly dancing over the keyboard. Pages of reports, deadlines, and plans were scattered around her, turning the dining table into an impromptu workstation.

Pete stood by the kitchen archway, watching her with a blend of admiration and concern. 'You've been at this for hours, Sarah. Come on, take a break.'

Sarah glanced up, her eyes meeting Pete's. 'I can't, Pete. These deadlines won't meet themselves.'

Pete moved closer, resting his hands gently on her shoulders. 'I understand you have commitments, but you also have a life outside of work. We had plans for tonight, remember?'

Sarah felt a sting of guilt. They had planned a simple date night, a brief interlude in their busy lives. 'I know, and

I'm really sorry. But this is important. We're talking about a promotion here, one that can set us up for the future.'

Pete sighed softly. 'I get it, the future is important. But so is the present, Sarah.'

'I know you understand why I'm doing this,' Sarah said, her voice tinged with hope and exhaustion. 'It's not just for me; it's for us, for our future.'

Pete bent down, planting a soft kiss on her forehead. 'I always understand, that's what I do. But don't forget, we also need to live for now.'

'Once this is over, we'll have all the time in the world. I promise,' she assured herself more than him, her eyes already drifting back to her laptop screen.

She snapped back to the present, the image of Pete's concerned face fading. *Oh, Pete. I bet you would have had all the right things to say about my accident.* The temptation to call him was overwhelming, yet she hesitated.

Her eyes refocused, the hotel room coming sharply back into focus. That promise was never fulfilled. The future she had toiled for was gone now. And so was Pete.

It's a door I closed, she reminded herself. *I can't just swing it back open because I'm feeling awful.* Her fingers hovered over her phone before retracting.

Another message from Benito appeared: *Don't worry about anything, okay? We'll sort it all out when I get there.*

His words were reassuring, but they weren't a balm for the type of ache she was feeling. Still, she had to admit, she was grateful for his effort. He might not be predictable like Pete, but he was willing to be there, to step in when she was down.

She lay there, her mind replaying the events that had led her to this solitary place, when a single truth emerged like a beacon in the fog: She had forfeited the right to lean on Pete the moment she walked away. The realization was a weight upon her chest, making it hard to breathe. Yet, within that weight was a release, a letting go of the what-ifs and the what-might-have-beens.

Was she ready to be fully independent, to be the sole architect of her adventures without the safety net of someone like Pete? Her recent mishap at Mag-aso Falls was a stark reminder of her vulnerability. Yet, it was also a testament to her survival, her ability to adapt and to overcome.

Sarah didn't need to call Pete. She didn't need to cling to a past that no longer fit the person she was becoming. Instead, she would step forward into the unknown, her heart open to whatever adventures lay ahead, her spirit unburdened by the ghosts of what once was.

With a deep, steadying breath, Sarah felt the tightness in her chest begin to ease. Life, she mused, was an endless series of twists and turns, some leading to incredible vistas and others to shadowed valleys. The unpredictability she had once craved for now seemed like a daunting path stretching out before her, each step a test of her resilience.

There was comfort in knowing Benito was on his way, his presence a reminder that she wasn't entirely alone in her journey. She was grateful for his company, for the assurance of a friend who understood her need for freedom, even as he watched over her with a protective eye.

A small smile found its way to Sarah's lips as she acknowledged her fears and doubts. They were part of her, but they did not define her. She forgave herself for the momentary yearning for the past, for the human need for connection that had momentarily made her feel weak.

She resolved then to make the most out of her trip, to embrace both the beauty and the bruises that came with living fully. Sarah would start her blog, share her stories, and maybe, just maybe, inspire someone else to chase their waterfalls, no matter how unpredictable the journey might be. She had found so much of herself during her journey. This was her way of giving back.

Her gaze drifted to the laptop beside her on the bed, the screen dark yet full of potential stories to tell. It would be her canvas, her way of connecting with the world while maintaining the independence she so cherished.

Life is a series of unpredictable moments. The thought repeated, something that needed to be written down. She grabbed her laptop and started typing the first draft post of her new blog, *Sarah, the Seeker.*

Captivating Kawasan Falls, she typed. As the words appeared on the screen, her heart felt lighter. There were many more waterfalls to see, many more experiences to capture, and a myriad of unpredictable people and events that would fill her life's chapters.

She looked at Benito's message again and wrote back: *Thanks, I'm looking forward to sorting it all out.*

For now, that would have to be enough. Sarah leaned back, her thoughts settling like the steady flow of water after a turbulent drop. She was right where she was supposed to be, warts and all.

When it comes to Benito and sleeping arrangements, I'll just wing it, she thought. With that, she closed her laptop, placed her phone back on the nightstand, and surrendered herself to the uncertainties of life, finding peace in her decision to move forward.

And as sleep finally began to claim her, it was with the knowledge that the path ahead was hers and hers alone. The waterfalls awaited, each one a chapter, each chapter a step towards the person she was meant to be. The story of Sarah was far from over, and it was one she was ready to write on her own terms.

CHAPTER 15

Sarah woke up to the shimmering rays of the morning sun seeping through the gaps of her hotel room curtains. She stretched her arms, feeling the tightness in her muscles from the previous day's ordeal at Mag-aso Falls. Her gaze drifted to her bandaged ankle propped up on a pillow at the foot of the bed. *Time for a new day,* she thought, *and a new adventure.*

Lying in her hotel bed, she could feel the dull ache from her fall as a constant reminder of her physical limitations. Yet, her mind was restless, eager to do what her body could not.

Sarah picked up her phone from the bedside table, reading another reassuring message from Benito: *Just touched down. Can't wait to join you.*

Smiling, she put down the phone and opened her laptop. It was high time she followed through on something she had been contemplating for a while: her own blog. Today, she would not venture into the lush greens and blues of the Philippines' waterfalls; instead, she'd dive into the digital realm to share her journey with the world.

Not just about waterfalls, but about all the adventures I'll have. The world is too big and life too short to limit my curiosity, she mused.

While she had a stand-in name from the previous night when she had written the draft of her first blog post, she pondered several other names; she thought about all the things that ended in her life. Now, she was seeking something new, something more aligned with who she was. *Sarah, the Seeker* it was, growing on her. The name had come naturally, just like her impulse to write about Kawasan Falls.

It's perfect.

Within an hour, she had set up her blog, matching Facebook page, and an Instagram account. She marvelled at how streamlined the process was—her tech-savvy side had its advantages. Her Facebook page would serve as a space for sharing longer updates and engaging with a community of waterfall enthusiasts. Her Instagram, @sarahtheseeker, would be a visual diary of her expeditions. She made a quick note in her journal about how she planned different angles and content for each page.

Sarah fine-tuned her digital presence, adjusting settings and double-checking links. With a sense of accomplishment, she prepared to write her first feature blog post. The topic was clear: Kawasan Falls, a place that still echoed in her mind with its roaring beauty and serene power.

She poised her fingers over the keyboard, hesitating for a moment. Before she could dive into the description of Kawasan Falls, she needed a moment to gather her memories and senses to translate the experience into words. With that in mind, she pulled away from her laptop for a brief respite, to read her journal, gather her thoughts, and ready herself for the vivid retelling that awaited.

Captivating Kawasan Falls, Cebu

Amid the verdant canopies of Cebu, where the sun plays hide and seek with the leaves, lies a spectacle of nature's artistry—Kawasan Falls. The journey to its basin is as much a part of the experience as the destination itself, with each step through the winding paths and each breath of the moist, earthy air heightening the sense of anticipation.

As I followed the trail, I could hear the distant sound of rushing water filling me with excitement. The sound grew to a crescendo, from a quiet murmur to a powerful roar, a clear call that I was nearing the heart of the falls. The air grew cooler, the mist more pronounced, and then, suddenly, the canopy parted to reveal the majestic cascade of Kawasan Falls.

The water was an astonishing shade of blue, reminiscent of a gemstone freshly unearthed. It cascaded down rocky tiers, each layer a different note in the harmonic masterpiece of the landscape. Each drop that hit the water's surface sent ripples that danced in the sunlight like liquid crystals.

The main pool is a natural amphitheatre, with water crashing down into it from the cliffs above, sending up plumes of spray that catch the light like diamonds against a sunbeam.

To stand in the basin of Kawasan Falls is to stand in the midst of a perpetual rainbow. The spray creates a fine mist that surrounds you, and as the sunlight filters through, the colours of the spectrum come alive.

I dipped my toe in, and the chill of the water sent a tingling sensation up my spine. The atmosphere was tranquil, only punctuated by the music of nature—the rustling leaves, chirping birds, and the constant hum of the waterfall. The latter is all-encompassing, a sound that reverberates through your body and insists on a moment of reverence.

Even the air had a unique character. It was thick with moisture but also refreshingly cool. Each breath I took felt cleansing, like inhaling the essence of the Earth itself.

The water was so inviting, cool, and refreshing against the skin, a welcome respite from the heat. Swimming in the pool beneath the falls, you're at the mercy of the current, pulled into the rhythm of the water. It was a powerful reminder of nature's gentle strength and untamed beauty.

As I left Kawasan Falls, the sensation of water droplets on my skin evaporated, but the imprint of the experience stayed with me. It was a reminder that sometimes the most beautiful places on earth require a journey, physical and spiritual, to truly understand their magnificence.

And, of course, let's not forget the local flavours. I thoroughly enjoyed my little picnic of lechon, pusó, and Coke. The lechon itself will be the topic of a totally different blog on its own. After that, sipping fresh coconut juice from a husk, the nutty sweetness perfectly complemented the sensory spectacle of Kawasan Falls.

So, why I did I go to Kawasan Falls in the first place? It's all thanks to @MaverickMarley [Check out her awesome blog here]. A month ago, I would never have dreamed of setting foot in these falls. My baby brother introduced me to Marley, hoping to cheer me up after a couple of setbacks (in life and in love). At first, I thought I just wanted to get moving, get fit. But it became more than that. After I visited Batlag Falls in Rizal and successfully completed my first river trail ride with her to Kinabuan Falls (also in Rizal), I was obsessed. There's just nothing like the exhilaration of finding a waterfall. It's never an easy hike. You have to go down a trail and go up again. But it doesn't matter. Just being in a waterfall basin is the best feeling in the world.

After Batlag and Kinabuan, I asked myself, 'What if I visited five more waterfalls?' Everyone said I was crazy.

But here I am.

I hope you, dear readers, can one day experience this wonder for yourselves. Until then, let's keep seeking the extraordinary in the ordinary world.

Happy travels,
Sarah, the Seeker

She read the blog post twice, making a few tweaks here and there. With the entry complete, Sarah felt a surge of satisfaction. She hoped her words would transport readers, giving them a taste of the awe that Kawasan Falls had instilled in her. She added her favourite photographs—snapshots that captured the blue hues of the water and the lush green surroundings. Finally, satisfied, she clicked the 'Publish' button. She also shared the blog post on her new Facebook and Instagram pages.

Well, that's that. The journey of a thousand miles—or posts—begins with a single click.

Sarah reclined, her gaze drifting from the screen to the world outside her window. The sky was bright with the midday sun. The entry was out there now, and all she could do was wait and see if it resonated with others as deeply as it did with her.

Before turning off her laptop, she couldn't resist refreshing her social media pages a few times. No likes or comments yet, but it was early.

Mentally exhausted, she drifted off into a nap, dreaming of waterfalls and her freshly launched blog.

Sarah woke up to a pleasant surprise. Her phone was abuzz with notifications. Her blog had gained followers, and the

Instagram and Facebook pages she'd linked to it had attracted some attention as well.

She was elated but also felt a tinge of pressure. *Can I sustain this? What if I can't keep up with their expectations?*

As she pondered, her eyes drifted to another text from Benito: *In an airport taxi now. Will reach you soon. Super excited for the adventure that awaits.*

Let's do this, she thought, already contemplating her next blog entry. She opened her laptop and began jotting down ideas for upcoming posts—travel tips, hidden spots in Bohol, and, of course, the story of Cambugahay Falls, where she would soon find herself accompanied by Benito.

Sarah took a deep breath and returned to her new blog, typing up an addendum to her first post:

Blog Update: A Note to My New Followers

Wow! I woke up from a nap to find that I have a small but growing community of followers. I'm beyond thrilled to share my adventures with all of you. Sure, there's a little pressure (okay, maybe a lot), but the excitement far outweighs it. My first entries will be about seven waterfalls that I'm currently chasing. Kawasan Falls isn't my first waterfall, it's my third! So, please don't expect my entries to be in chronological order. I'll be referring to my trusty journal as I backtrack and fast forward. However, this is just the beginning. Here's to more wonders and untold adventures! Let the journey continue!

Yours truly,
Sarah, the Seeker

Sarah pressed 'Publish' again, her heart pounding but her spirit buoyant. She was ready for whatever came next.

Her next task was to write an 'About' section for her blog. The text was concise and direct, inviting readers to join her as she revisited her travels through words and images. It wasn't long before she found her rhythm, her fingers confidently tapping away as she laid the foundation of her online persona.

As she set aside her laptop and began to tidy up her hotel room, her thoughts returned to Benito, soon to be by her side, and to the other adventures that awaited them both.

Life is unpredictable, she mused. *But that's the beauty of it. And now, I get to share this unpredictable, wondrous life with the world.*

Sarah's excitement had clearly gotten the better of her. And for the first time in a long while, she wouldn't have it any other way.

CHAPTER 16

A knock on the door, and Sarah knew it was Benito. She hobbled over to the door to open it. Before any words were spoken, she got a bear hug. Sarah was prepared to feel any number of things about Benito showing up at her door, but happiness was the first thing she felt and the last thing she expected.

'First I have to take a look at that leg injury,' Benito said. At first, Sarah felt awkward about showing her ankle to him. *But it was Benito!* She lay her right leg on the bed so he could have a better look.

'Actually, it's an ankle injury,' Sarah clarified. 'No fracture, no inflamed tendon,' she told him.

'It looks nasty, though.'

It really was. There was a deep gash above her ankle and the area around it was already black and blue. Worst of all, it really felt like hell.

'Okay, the first thing we're going to do is change accommodations.'

'No way! I can't afford anything fancier than this place,' Sarah replied. Her hotel was decent and clean. That was all she needed.

'Um, nope, I'm not staying here. Not when we can stay at Preciosa Costa.'

Preciosa Costa? She had spent at least thirty minutes drooling over the villas on their website before moving on to more practical accommodations in Panglao Island. And did he say *we?*

'What?'

'You heard me. We're transferring to Preciosa Costa. Time to check out.'

'I'm not allowing you to spend for me,' Sarah said. She stuck out her chin for emphasis.

'Sarah! My dad's friend owns the place. He was the one who told me that I could stay at Preciosa for free. So, don't argue any more. Who can argue with free?'

Sarah shrugged. He did have a point.

'C'mon, I'll help you pack.'

'No, no, no. I have a system.'

'Let me help! You're injured!'

'Let's not have a shouting match over how helpful you are,' Sarah said as she crossed her arms.

'Okay, fine. Also, Preciosa is a better place for you to recover.'

'You're preaching to the choir. I've actually checked out Preciosa Costa before and it looked really gorgeous. My only problem was the budget.'

'Well, it's not a problem any more.'

Sarah smiled as she packed her bags. She told Benito to go ahead to the lobby. She wasn't going to let him touch her clothes (and underwear!). Also, there wasn't much to pack, anyway.

'Omigod, Benito,' Sarah said as they got to their ocean-view villa. It had its own living room, dining area, plunge pool, and a private balcony overlooking the Bohol Sea. Sarah wasn't used to this kind of luxury. She couldn't believe how lucky she was. It was a total upgrade from her standard double room.

'It's beautiful, isn't it? You can just laze around for one whole day here. Just relax. I don't want you moving on to your next itinerary with that ankle of yours.'

'But can we go to Siquijor tomorrow?'

'Fine. But just rest today. Okay?'

'Okay. Um, Benito?'

'Yeah?'

'There's only one bed.'

'No shit, Sherlock!'

'I'm serious. Are you making this into a joke?'

'You take the king-size bed. I'll take the little daybed over there, near the desk.'

'But, Benito, you're not going to get any sleep on that little sofa.' Sarah was trying not to look but he looked gorgeous in a grey dri-fit shirt that emphasized his broad shoulders and muscled pecs. Benito was tall and brawny. He was going to fall right off that teeny-weeny daybed. Why was it even called a 'bed'? It looked more like a couch.

'I can ask the staff for an extra bed.'

'But that might cost us extra,' Sarah considered. 'Well, this is a big bed . . .'

Sarah started to blush, but she made sure he didn't see her face. She bent her head low and pretended to unpack her bag (there wasn't much to unpack, though).

'Are you going to take advantage of me, Sarah Silvestre?'

'Benito!' Sarah threw a pillow at him.

'That settles it. I'm going for a swim. You rest here. Keep that leg on the bed, okay? I'll ring the front desk for an ice pack,' Benito said as he started taking off his shirt. It was like he did it every day in front of Sarah. She was shocked into immobility. She tried looking at the ceiling, at the plunge pool outside the room, but it was no good. Her eyes were drawn to his abs. In all the years they'd been friends, she didn't remember a time that she had gotten a good look at them.

'Is something wrong?'

'What?' Sarah's brain didn't seem to be working.

'You're looking at me funny.'

'No, nothing's wrong.' But it did feel *a little wrong* to be looking at his body the way she did.

'Just go swim already,' she said. She was angry with herself for feeling confused. *They were just friends.*

It was even worse for Sarah when he came back with wet hair and body. He towelled himself off in the room like it was nobody's business.

'Could you please cover up a bit?'

'Jeez, Sarah. I didn't realize you were such a manang.' He got the complimentary terry towel robe in the closet and put it on. 'Unless you're getting turned on or something,' he teased.

'Ugh, Benito.' She *was* getting turned on. It was hard to admit, though.

'Get dressed already. Let's have some dinner at The Safflower. My treat!'

'I didn't bring a lot of clothes. I'll have to wear what I'm wearing,' she said, indicating her shirt and shorts.

'That's fine. You look great, whatever you wear.' Did Benito just compliment her? Sarah smiled to herself.

The restaurant was beside the infinity pool. As Sarah looked out at the darkening sky, she couldn't think of a better place to be. They had a delicious seafood dinner and some white wine. After dinner, Benito asked her if she was up for a walk along Alona Beach. Preciosa Costa was at the top of a limestone cliff overlooking Alona Beach. Sarah felt well rested and her ankle was feeling better after the cold compress.

'I'm glad I'm here with you, Sarah,' Benito began.

'Me too, actually.'

'I have a surprise for you!'

'What is it?'

'Check this out,' he said, handing her a brochure with a map of Siquijor. 'It was at the lobby.'

Sarah took a look at the highlights: a natural spring at the base of an ancient-looking tree, a beach with white sand, and, best of all, waterfalls!

Benito smiled. 'I've booked a guide to take us around Siquijor tomorrow.'

'Wow, thank you so much!'

'It would be a pity if we didn't go around Siquijor. It's so small, I think we could go around the whole island in an hour.'

'You think?'

'Yeah! I hear it's a really tiny island.'

'What time are we leaving tomorrow?'

'Let's see,' Benito said, turning over the brochure to check out the ferry schedule, 'The first fast ferry is heading out to Siquijor at 10.00 a.m.'

'Okay, we'd better sleep early then.'

'Did you know that Siquijor is rumoured to be a haven for witches?' Benito pointed to one of the photos on the brochure. 'Look at that. They sell love potions in souvenir shops.' True enough, there were glass bottles with what seemed like oil and herbs mixed together and labelled as 'love potions'.

'I don't believe in those things.'

'I do.'

Sarah was surprised. She'd known him since forever, but she was still discovering new things about him.

'Really?'

'I think the supernatural is just as real as anything natural. It's the same thing as believing that we have souls.'

'That's true. I didn't see it that way.'

'I think it's possible to be bewitched.'

Sarah laughed. Knowing how many girlfriends he'd had in the past, she wasn't surprised.

'What? What's so funny?'

'You've had so many girlfriends, it's not hard to believe!'

'I haven't had that many girlfriends.'

'Really? Ask me how many boyfriends I've had.'

'I know the answer to that. There was just Pete. So, how many girlfriends have I had?'

Sarah held up six fingers, 'Pinky in your junior year of high school. Then there was Charmaine in your senior year, but you went ahead and charmed another girl, Jessica. So, I count them separately, even though you technically cheated on one of them.'

'Hey! I was young and stupid—'

'I'm not done! Then there was Samantha from freshman to sophomore year of college, followed by Eliza in your junior year, on and off, until senior year. I thought you would stick with Eliza. But then you broke up with her and went out with Gia, the model. Two years with Gia and then you broke up with her. That's it!'

'You remember every single one of them?'

They were best friends, weren't they?

'Yup. Trust me, Benito. You really are easily bewitched.'

Benito gave her a look that, for once, she couldn't read.

'Sarah?' Benito called. It was the middle of the night. Somehow, Sarah couldn't sleep after their conversation. It turned out, neither could Benito.

'Yes?'

'Were you serious about sharing the bed?'

'I told you. You really don't fit on that couch, do you?'

'No.'

'Well, come here, then. I'll set up the pillows between us.'

'Do you really have to do that? It's just me, Sarah.'

Sarah's heart beat loudly in her chest. It wasn't him she didn't trust. Sarah couldn't trust herself with Benito in the same bed with her.

'Okay, whatever,' Sarah said.

She heard him move from the couch to the bed, in the darkness.

'Good night.'

'Good night.'

Sarah did not get much sleep that night. She was too aware of Benito's body lying practically a foot away from her.

Sarah woke up with Benito's arm thrown across her chest, over her shoulder. It didn't feel awkward to her. Just right, just natural. She gently moved his arm back to his side and shook his shoulder.

'Get up, sleepy head. We have to catch the earliest boat out to Siquijor, remember?'

Benito groaned in response.

The two-hour trip to Siquijor was pleasant and quick for Sarah because she had Benito to talk to the whole time. Jun, their tour guide, met them at the port area. Benito told him that their main itinerary was Cambugahay Falls. The rest would be optional.

They hired a tricycle for their whole-day tour and started heading towards Lazi, where the falls were located.

'You can't miss the balete tree,' Jun informed them. 'It's not far from Cambugahay and it's near the main road.'

Jun wasn't kidding. The tricycle stopped by the side of the road, and they were greeted by the beautiful sight of a huge balete tree with a pool of clear water at its base. The water was coming from a natural spring and the people from Lazi dammed the stream with concrete, turning it into a public pool.

'Go ahead, take a dip,' Jun said. There weren't any other people with them. Sarah and Benito enjoyed sitting along the edge of the pool, their feet immersed in the cool water of the spring.

'How's your ankle?'

'It's okay, Benito. Don't worry about it.'

They went back to the tricycle refreshed. They weren't far from Cambugahay Falls. Just like Mag-aso Falls, there was a downhill climb. Sarah was glad that Benito was with her. He helped her negotiate the stone stairs. She felt the familiar excitement of hearing the falls first before seeing them. Jun told them he would watch over their things while they swam.

When they finally reached the bottom of what seemed like endless stairs, Sarah wanted to jump in right away. The water was green and inviting and the falls were multi-layered this time, with three major catch basins.

'Careful,' Benito warned. He helped her balance on the rocks before she fully immersed herself in the water. It was like heaven. The water was warm and the falls were gentler and lower than the one at Mag-aso. They lounged in the biggest of the lagoons before exploring the other levels.

'Hey, there's a vine for jumping over here!' Benito called out. She saw him swing from the vine and splash into the water.

'I want to do it, too!' Sarah shouted.

'Nope. You have an injury. We'll have to come back here one of these days.'

'We really have to!' Sarah laughed. Benito bellowed like Tarzan on his next jump.

They spent a good hour discovering the other lagoons and smaller falls. Sarah picked up another small pebble from her fifth waterfall. It was smooth and white.

After Cambugahay Falls, they still made it to Salagdoong Beach where Benito did a cliff dive (Sarah was happy to just watch) before heading back to the port.

Journal entry
Fifth Stop: Cambugahay Falls

Cambugahay Falls was three tiers of pure joy. Located in Siquijor, each level had its own swimming area. The water was as clear as crystal and as cool as a gentle breeze. Watching my friend swinging off a rope into the water, I felt like a child without a care in the world. Next time I'm here, I want to try that too.

Small, white pebble.

A good friend makes the journey so much easier.

CHAPTER 17

'I don't understand why you're so insistent about this,' Benito said, frowning. They'd been arguing all through dinner at The Safflower. It would have been the perfect day for Sarah if only it hadn't ended with Benito telling her that she shouldn't proceed with her plan to go to Iligan.

'It's *my* dream adventure. I'm glad you're here. I'm glad we got to stay at Preciosa. But you can't tell me it ends here. I'm going all the way to Lake Sebu whether you like it or not.'

'Sarah, I have a few family friends in Iligan. But that's it. I can't guarantee that we'll be safe. Aren't you concerned about safety at all? It's unstable over there. Armed conflicts could happen without warning.'

'Well, for a rich kid like you, yeah. Safety first. But I can blend in, Benito. No one's going to ransom me for *my* money.' There, she said it: her secret judgement of her own friend. She said it because she was angry. She said it because her anger made her careless.

Benito's face looked like she had just slapped him. She immediately regretted what she had just said. But words are slippery. And when they are out, no one can reel them back in.

'I'm sorry, Benito.'

She knew it was too late.

'I'm going for a walk' was all Benito said. He was too nice to take on her mud-slinging. But he was too upset to finish dinner with her.

It was close to midnight by the time Benito got back to the villa. Sarah knew because she counted every minute since he left The Safflower to 'take a walk'.

'Benito?'

Silence greeted her. She was prepared for a fight, but she wasn't prepared for silence.

'Benito, please talk to me,' Sarah said. She was close to tears.

'What do you want me to say?' Benito's voice was surprisingly tender.

'I'm really sorry.'

'But is that what you really think of me?'

'I didn't mean it.'

'So, what *did* you mean?'

She could see his profile in the dark. He was calm. He wasn't mad. His face was unreadable. But she did notice one thing: that he was incredibly handsome. She felt like she had been blind for many years. No, she'd always known. She had just been in denial the whole time. All of this flooded her mind as she tried to come up with a coherent answer to his question.

'I'm just an insecure little whiner, down on her luck, who doesn't deserve you as a friend.'

'No, that's not who you are.'

'Benito, I just didn't want you to think that I needed rescuing, okay? That's all. I'm capable. I'm angry that you don't trust me, that you don't trust my judgement. But I had no right to say all those things,' Sarah said through her tears.

Benito rushed to her side.

'Please don't cry because of me,' he said. He already had a box of tissues with him. It was a miracle how he managed to move so fast and still navigate in the dark for tissues. 'The last thing I want you to do is cry.'

'I deserve it.'

'Sarah, I know you're capable. I know you don't need to be rescued. I didn't mean for it to sound like that. I'm just genuinely scared about the safety situation in Iligan. That's all.' Benito reached out and held her hands in his. All of a sudden, Sarah felt a rush of emotions and sensations. His hands were warm, and she could feel his forearms. Just a few inches more and she could actually embrace him. She couldn't move. And she couldn't deny how nervous she felt at his touch. This was something different in all her years of friendship with Benito.

Am I falling in love with him? She didn't know the answer. She didn't want to know.

Benito pulled her closer into an embrace. Sarah did not resist. The next thing she knew, Benito was kissing the tears on her cheeks and then his mouth was on hers. It was a mind-blowing kiss. Sarah's thoughts flew out of her head and all she could feel was the incredible sensation of his lips on hers. His muscled arms were suddenly around her waist. His hands gently moved up and down her back as his tongue slowly parted her lips. A sweet ache moved through Sarah, from between her legs, spreading upwards to her already sensitive nipples. Sarah met his kiss, her tongue exploring his as well. His hands expertly unhooked her bra and moved from her back to her waist, slowly lifting her shirt up. As he was kissing her, his hands cupped her breasts, and his thumbs were circling her nipples. Sarah moaned. It was all too fast, but she didn't want him to stop.

His mouth left hers but, in an instant, they were on her breasts. At this point, Sarah was already on her back, on the bed. Benito hungrily took one nipple in his mouth while his other hand gently circled and massaged her other breast. Sarah could not believe the amount of pleasure she was feeling. She lifted her hips and moulded herself against him. She felt him grow hard.

Sarah's brain belatedly kicked in. *What am I doing? Why have I not been thinking?*

'Benito, wait,' Sarah said. She put her hands in his hair. Even his hair felt luxurious in her hands.

'What? What's the matter?' Benito replied. He was hovering above her now. She knew it was an effort for him to talk.

'What's going to happen?'

'Do you want me to stop, Sarah?' he whispered. He was daring her. His hands were still moving up and down her torso.

'No . . .' But it was a whisper. And it sounded like a question. Sarah wasn't so sure she had all her faculties intact.

Benito sensed her hesitation. He stopped moving, and all she could hear was their breathing.

'Benito, I'm sorry. This was all so sudden.'

'No, it's my fault, Sarah,' he said. He had already pulled away from her. She knew he was doing the right thing, but she wanted to go back into his arms. 'I don't want it to be like this. I don't want you to regret anything.'

But I don't regret it.

She heard him get up and go into the bathroom. She heard the shower turn on.

What just happened?

Sarah turned on a desk lamp to get her bearings. She retraced what happened. She had said something insensitive and stupid. He took a walk. When he came back, she had apologized. She was in tears. And then one thing led to another.

Or, did it go way back?

Seven years ago

It was her prom night at her all-girls' high school and she didn't want to go because she didn't have a date. Anya tried to convince her to go with her date's cousin, but Sarah wouldn't hear of it.

Two nights before her prom, Benito called her.

'Anya told me.'

'Yeah? What'd she tell you?'

'That you won't go to your prom.'

'It's no big deal. I don't believe in prom. It's overrated.'

'How can you tell it's overrated if you actually haven't been to one?'

'What's your point?'

'You should go.'

'You mean I should go stag? I don't know. I'd go stag if Anya didn't have a stupid date.'

'You should go with me.'

Sarah laughed out loud.

'What? Are you nuts? What would Charmaine say?'

'I'm already going to *her* school prom. Besides, she knows you're one of my best friends.'

'Are you serious, Benito? You're not just kidding around?'

'Why would I kid around about something as serious as prom?'

'It's just a prom. And I'm glad I won't have to spend on a silly dress.'

'But I already have a suit to wear.'

'Well, you'll really have to wear one for your grad ball.'

'What a waste of a good suit if I'll only wear it once.'

'Okay, not the most convincing argument to go to a prom.'

'Come with me, Sarah. We'll have a blast.'

'I don't know . . .' Sarah hesitated.

'You have absolutely nothing to lose. It'll be like having another fun night hanging out with one of your best friends, only we'll be in fancier clothes!'

'Well, now that you put it that way . . .'

'Is that a yes?'

'Fine.'

'Yes!'

Her mom panicked over having to get a dress just the day before prom, but they settled on one of her mom's old dresses. She took out her dependable sewing machine (that was how she had saved a lot on clothes) and adjusted it to Sarah's size. It was a chiffon, knee-length, halter-neck dress in an old rose colour with a black velvet belt that cinched the waist. Her mom took care of her make-up.

'Ate, you look very, very pretty,' Miguel said with a wide smile. She hugged her brother. She didn't want to look in her mom's direction yet because she could see her mom wiping the corners of her eyes with tissue. Then they all heard the doorbell.

'Hi, Tita Helen, you look gorgeous as usual,' Benito greeted her mom.

'You are looking very handsome in your suit!' her mom exclaimed.

'Your mom told me that you'd be wearing pink,' Benito said to her and smiled. He was holding a white and pink orchid corsage.

'Awww! You didn't have to, Benito,' Sarah said.

'Of course I had to! You're one of my best friends!' Her mom took a *lot* of pictures. Sarah still had the album full of those photos, even the ones with Miguel photo-bombing them.

They rode his dad's chauffeur-driven black car to her school. The gymnasium looked transformed with fairy lights greeting guests at the entrance. Well, the theme was Wonderland, after all. There was a photo wall where students could have their pictures taken. They took some wacky shots while waiting for Anya and her date, Sean, to show up.

They spent the whole night laughing, talking, and dancing. Sarah did not expect it to be so much fun. As curfew approached, Benito asked her if she wanted to take a walk along the track field just outside the gymnasium. She said yes.

The sky was dotted with stars as she and Benito headed out.

'Did you have fun?'

'Yes, I did. Thanks for asking me to prom. I would have missed all of this.'

'That was the point, you know.'

'I hope you have just as much fun at your grad ball and Charmaine's prom too.'

Benito was quiet.

'Sarah?'

'Yup?'

'Thanks to you, too, for saying yes.'

'I wouldn't say no to my best friend.'

He took her arm in his and they walked in companionable silence. Sarah remembered that it was a magical night. She thought it was a pleasant evening. That was it. Except for one strange thing. As they headed back to the gymnasium, Benito bent over and kissed her cheek. It definitely wasn't just a beso-beso for sure. She gave him a weird look, but he just had a mysterious smile on his face.

It was that smile that Sarah was remembering. *Was it that long ago?*

'Sarah?' Benito was dressed in a shirt and shorts already. His short hair was wet from the shower.

'I don't know what to say,' she was looking down at the blanket on the bed. She didn't want things to be awkward but awkward it was.

'You don't have to say anything. I'm sorry if that was too much for you.' *Too much? Or not enough?*

'It was . . . overwhelming.'

'Sarah . . . I don't know if you've ever noticed, but I've been waiting for you to be finally single.'

Everything came rushing to her head. The past few weeks he'd been hanging out at her house, that weird kiss at prom night, the many girlfriends he'd had.

'Why didn't you just come out and say so?'

'I've been dying to. I wasn't sure if you were over Pete. Ugh. I'm sorry. I did this all wrong.'

'Is it why you've been wanting to come with me on my waterfall trip?'

He just smiled.

'Benito?'

'Yes.'

'How long exactly—have you been waiting, I mean?'

'A very long time.'

'As early as my senior prom night?'

'Well, you said your mom didn't allow you to have a boyfriend.'

That was true.

'Honestly, Sarah?' He was looking into her eyes. Even though he was several feet away, she could feel the intensity of his look. 'Earlier than that.'

Sarah's mind was blown.

'The question is: do we go on or do we go home?' Benito asked.

'You don't want me to go to Iligan,' Sarah reminded him.

'It doesn't mean we can't go somewhere else. Why don't we go to Camiguin instead?' She was, all of a sudden, liking the 'we'.

'We can go to Camiguin?'

'We can go to Katibawasan Falls. And, I have relatives in Cagayan de Oro.'

'Well, where do you not have relatives, right?'

'Iligan.'

'You have a point.'

'And what about us?' Benito asked. *Tough question.*

'Can we take it one waterfall at a time?'

'So, it's a go?'

'Yes.'

CHAPTER 18

In the depth of night, Sarah lay in the dark, her eyes open, tracing the vague contours of the ceiling fan as it cut through the air.

It was Sarah's turn to be restless. When she heard Benito gently snoring on the daybed across from her king-size bed, she had to take a walk on her own. The swirling vortex of thoughts about the day's events, their heated argument turned passionate encounter, and the seismic shift in her relationship with Benito had her mind buzzing. She watched him as he lay there, sleeping with a serenity that contrasted sharply with her restless energy.

Quietly, she slipped out of the sheets and tiptoed out of the room. The door closed softly behind her. The beach at night was a world away from the bright, noisy bustle of daylight hours. It was a shadow realm where the sky met the sea, and the whispers of the waves spoke of mysteries.

She walked towards the beach, her bare feet sinking into the cool sand. The waves washed up on the shore rhythmically, a tranquil symphony conducted by the moon. It was as though the ocean understood her restlessness and was whispering for her to sit and confide her thoughts.

Finding a solitary spot, she sat down and hugged her knees, her gaze lost in the horizon where the dark sea kissed the starry sky, as if to hold together the pieces of her identity that the night seemed determined to unravel. The ocean's breath was warm against her skin, contrasting with the chill of her thoughts. She had always found solace in predictability; in the control she wielded over her life's direction. Yet, as she pondered the enigma that was Benito, she found herself stepping into the past.

She felt like her life had come to a juncture, one with no signposts, where each path led to an uncertain future.

She thought about her father, a man who had been always too busy chasing ambitions to pause and look around at what he already had. A man who worked long hours, not out of necessity, but because it was a part of who he was—restless, hungry for challenges, and perhaps a bit reckless. Her mother, left alone for long periods, had sought warmth in another relationship, culminating in a separation that had jolted Sarah's world when she was just seven.

She had spent years blaming her father for his neglect, for prioritizing work over family. Yet, here she was, doing something similar. Like her father, she had a fierce streak of independence, an untamed spirit that hated feeling boxed in. This spiritedness was perhaps her most significant inheritance from him, and as she sat there, she felt a grudging acceptance of that fact. Her work, much like his, demanded her all, but it also cost her—the costs were evident.

Did I turn into him? she wondered. *Is that such a bad thing?*

She couldn't shake the understanding that her father's absence was a blueprint she had subconsciously adopted. The realization stung with the sharpness of betrayal. It wasn't just her father's choices that had broken up her home. What if her dad hadn't been so driven? Maybe her parents would still be together. In the pursuit of success, had she forsaken something more important?

In the presence of the vast night sky, Sarah felt a cosmic insignificance. This feeling gave her silent permission to acknowledge her flaws, to see herself as a reflection of her father—driven, but neglectful.

Her mind then flickered to Benito. Until recently, he had occupied a fixed space in her life—as a friend, a confidant, a consistent presence. That night, the dynamic had shifted irrevocably. While the change surprised her, it wasn't unwelcome. Unlike Pete, Benito was a wildfire, sometimes volatile, and deeply passionate about certain things.

Benito had a hot-headed side, a fiery temper that she'd seen flare up before. That temper, though he had done his best to suppress it, had led to their argument. It was also that same intensity that made him excited about the things and people he loved. It was this emotional fervour that she had found lacking in her life recently, and she couldn't help but admire it, even if it came with its set of challenges.

Benito, who had stood steadfastly by her side as a friend, now emerged in her heart's eye as a lover—unpredictable, yet strangely right. Her mind sifted through memories of him, seeing not just the companion but the man whose hidden depths she had only just begun to explore. The contrast was stark when she thought of Pete.

Benito's spontaneity, which once exasperated her, now drew her in with the allure of the unknown. His adventurous spirit promised not a smooth and steady path, but one filled with the vibrancy of uncharted territories. With him, life felt like a series of waves—unpredictable, powerful, each one a new adventure.

And yet, there was that fire within him, a hot-headedness that matched her own fierce independence. Could two such flames burn close without scorching each other? She pondered whether their passionate natures would lead to conflicts, or if, perhaps, they could find a way to dance together, creating a harmony in the heat.

She admired his passion. It was a trait that scared her in its intensity but also called to something primal within her. With Benito, she saw the possibility of a partnership that could withstand storms, his fire complementing her resolve, his spontaneity challenging her structure.

She glanced back at the sky, taking in the breathtaking array of stars shining in the darkness. It was an awe-inspiring display just for her, on this particular night, when she had so much to contemplate. It was a night to fall in love, and she was overwhelmingly grateful that Benito had revealed his long-concealed feelings for her.

It was a feeling both terrifying and exhilarating, like standing at the edge of a cliff, the ocean below beckoning her to leap. There was an undeniable magic in the air. Sarah breathed in deeply, the scent of the sea mingling with that of the earth, grounding her as her thoughts soared.

She felt something stir inside her, a feeling unacknowledged until now. Happiness. It bloomed within her. Slowly, steadily.

Smiling, she thought about their upcoming trip to Camiguin, about the waterfalls they'd be seeing, the experiences they'd share. But more than the physical journey, she was excited about the emotional expedition they were about to embark on.

Finally, with a sense of clarity settling inside her, she stood up and made her way back to the villa. Benito was still lost in sleep, oblivious to her existential wanderings. She carefully climbed back into bed.

As she closed her eyes, her thoughts drifted back to her father. Maybe they were similar, but that didn't mean they had to make the same mistakes. With that comforting thought, she finally let sleep envelop her, carrying her into dreams filled with waterfalls, wild adventures, and new beginnings.

CHAPTER 19

Benito did his best to make the morning after not so awkward. He had opted to sleep on the daybed the night before. He had a cup of coffee ready for Sarah when she got up early the next morning.

'I have good news and I have bad news,' Benito announced.

'Okay, bad news first.'

'The ferry ride is going to take four hours.'

Sarah remembered the two-hour ride from Siquijor to Bohol. It was going to be double that. It *was* bad news.

'The good news is we don't have to pass through Cagayan de Oro. We can go straight to Camiguin from Tagbilaran! For the longest time, there weren't any ferries between Bohol and Camiguin. But apparently, the service is back. We have to leave right now. And if we're lucky, we might see dolphins on the way to Camiguin.'

They started packing their stuff immediately. The rush allowed Sarah to temporarily forget about everything that had happened the night before. But as soon as they were on the ferry, with time on their hands, Sarah couldn't help but reflect on what had happened between her and Benito (or what might have happened).

Sarah surreptitiously inspected Benito's profile. It was the same Benito, the one who had always been her friend. But he was different too. She'd always known that other girls easily fell for him. She wasn't immune. It was just that she was always so busy with her studies. And then Pete came along.

In the six years that she and Pete were a couple, Sarah never went as far as she did with Benito. It was partly because she had set the terms early in their relationship. And it was partly because she wanted to avoid what had happened to her mother. Her mother had married early. Too early in Sarah's opinion. She had gotten pregnant straight out of college and there was no other recourse for her mother but to marry her father. That didn't turn out so well.

Sarah was on the pill 'just in case'. She was that much of a control freak. She had never really needed it, anyway, with Pete. Maybe that was why he ended up with what's-her-name? Joanna. Maybe he was getting some. Maybe six years was just too long a wait for some men. And maybe Sarah wasn't worth the wait for Pete.

All of that control just flew out the window in one night. Had she gone crazy? Or was this because she was altogether a different Sarah now?

'Sarah?' Benito touched her arm. His touch was different now. Her skin crackled with electricity. Sarah wondered if Benito could feel it too.

'Are you over-analysing last night?' he asked. He was smiling a lopsided smile.

All of a sudden, Sarah could catalogue all of Benito's smiles. Her memory was rich with them. She wanted to hoard each one of them.

'What are we now?'

'That's a good question. What do you want us to be?'

'I'm scared that I'll lose a friend.'

'That will never happen.'

'Yes, I will. As soon as this turns into something else, you won't be the best friend you used to be.' Sarah's voice caught towards the end. It was true. It was one of the most precious things to her. She didn't want things to change. But they already had.

They were on the deck of the ferry and the wind was blowing her hair into her face. Benito gently traced his finger across her cheek, drawing away her hair from her face, and tucking it behind her ear.

'I'm taking the same chance too. I want to do this the right way. I want to win you over. But I want this to be your choice, Sarah.'

Was it a choice when she felt heady with desire just standing next to him?

'All I know is I still want you by my side on this trip, Benito.'

'That's good enough for me.'

Sarah smiled.

'Look!' Benito called out. First, they just saw one and then two bottlenose dolphins jumping by the ferry. Then they saw a whole pod of them, their silvery grey bodies glistening in the late morning sun. Sarah tried taking a photo with her phone, but it came out a little blurry. It didn't matter. It was a beautiful sight. She was glad she shared the dolphin sighting with Benito.

'I wish I had taken a better photo,' Sarah said.

'Will this do?' Benito showed her his snap. It showed her smiling profile, her hair blowing around her face, watching the dolphins. Was that how he saw her?

'It's perfect.'

They rode the hotel van to the Parao Resort where they made reservations. This time, they got a room with a queen-size bed and a single bed. At the resort, they made a deal with a habal-habal driver to take them to Katibawasan and from there to some hot springs, within the same day, and then drop them back to the resort. Camiguin Island was smaller than Siquijor, so a day trip between Katibawasan Falls and Ardent Hot Springs was manageable.

After dropping off their stuff in the room, they left for the Falls. It took them only twenty minutes to get to Katibawasan Falls.

The falls dropped a good 250 feet into a clear green rock pool. The driver explained to them on the way to Katibawasan Falls that the pool was at the foot of Mt Timpoong and that the clean water came from the cold springs of the mountain.

Sarah and Benito were glad for the cool water because the noon sun had been beating down on them. For Sarah, it wasn't the most dramatic of the waterfalls she'd seen. But, still, it was one of the most peaceful. Sarah had to dip herself slowly in the water because it was just that cold. Eventually, her body temperature adjusted. As Sarah swam towards the centre of the pool, she saw some swallows fly close to the water, skimming the surface. Not far from her was Benito. She couldn't think of a more perfect moment.

After their swim, they ate some crispy kiping, a local delicacy made of cassava served with latik or coconut milk syrup, as they marvelled at the lush ferns and orchids that surrounded the emerald pool. Sarah picked up her sixth pebble. This one was grey with streaks of white and green.

After they had dried themselves off, they rode the habal-habal for another twenty minutes to get to Ardent Springs.

This time, the springs were hidden away from the sun, underneath the canopy of high trees and fishing nets (that kept the pool clear from dropping leaves). The pool was developed. It reminded Sarah of the way the locals in Siquijor had dammed the freshwater spring at the foot of the balete tree. There were concrete steps leading to the hot stream.

They were told to take it slowly. The hottest of the pools was forty degrees centigrade, the same temperature as a high fever. They couldn't just plunge into the water. They had to slowly wade in and adjust their body temperature one section at a time.

'This is going to be therapeutic for your ankle, Sarah,' Benito said.

'I'm feeling it!'

The water felt heavenly to Sarah. And the pools were invigorating. There were six pools all in all. The third one had a lovely mini waterfall that she could just not get enough of. The fourth pool was the hottest of all but still just as enjoyable.

While Sarah was a little disappointed that she didn't get to see Tinago Falls in Iligan, she felt that both Katibawasan Falls and Ardent Hot Springs more than made up for it.

'The heat is coming from Mt Hibok-Hibok,' Benito explained to Sarah. 'Did you know that it's an active volcano?'

'No. That's amazing!'

Because it was a weekday, Sarah and Benito had the pools all to themselves for the afternoon. Sarah basked in the delicious and therapeutic heat of the pools.

They discussed the lore of the hot springs, how locals revered the spot for its restorative powers, and some even claimed a spiritual connection to the land because of it. For Sarah, it was a reminder of nature's ability to provide sanctuary, not just for wildlife, but for the human soul as well.

Time seemed irrelevant in the embrace of the hot springs, but eventually, Sarah and Benito acknowledged the need to move on. They left the comfort of the water, albeit reluctantly, their skin tingling and hearts warmed by the earth's generosity.

Journal entry
Sixth Stop: Katibawasan Falls

Next on my journey was Katibawasan Falls in Camiguin. Standing at 250 feet, this waterfall was a sight to behold. The pool at its base was shallow but immensely refreshing, and the ferns surrounding the falls added an extra layer of serenity.

Grey stone, with streaks of white and green.

Desire is hard to cool.

CHAPTER 20

'How's your ankle?' Benito asked Sarah.

'Much better. I think the hot springs did some magic!'

'Let's take a walk?' Benito beckoned. It was sunset and the beach looked inviting. Sarah nodded. She thought of the night before and the night ahead. Butterflies fluttered in her stomach.

'You know, we could end the trip here. You've already seen a lot and been through a lot.'

'Benito, I said seven waterfalls. That's my goal. And Seven Falls is the best of them all. I mean, it's at Lake Sebu. It's beautiful!'

'You're so stubborn!' he said, but he was smiling.

'Tenacious,' Sarah corrected him.

'Well, that's one of the reasons why . . .' he paused, and took her hand in his.

Sarah's skin prickled at his touch. She couldn't deny it to herself any more. There was something electric between them, something that was definitely not on the platonic level. She didn't let go of his hand.

'Sarah, I've had the best time with you.'

'So have I.'

'And I want to know,' he hesitated a bit, but continued, 'I want to know, now, if I have a chance with you.' He wasn't looking at her, though, as if afraid to hear her answer.

Sarah was touched. In all the years that she'd known him, this was the first time she was seeing the confident, jokey Benito looking the most vulnerable. She wanted to put her hands on his face and make him turn to look her in the eye. But she was scared too.

'Hey,' Sarah replied, 'look at me.'

He turned to look at her, and she knew it. She knew that she was feeling exactly what he was feeling. She felt a familiar ache growing in her stomach and spreading across her body.

'Benito, I want to be with you.'

He leaned forward and kissed her on the lips. She kissed him back, aware of how close they were, of how he smelled like soap and musk, of how incredible his skin felt against hers.

They were in their room before they knew it. This time, there was no confusion over what would happen next. They couldn't keep their hands off each other. Sarah didn't know how they managed to be locked in a kiss while getting undressed, but they managed the feat.

'Are you safe?' Benito asked, his face serious.

'I'm on the pill,' she said. Not the most romantic thing to say to each other but at least they got it out of the way.

Benito laid her on the bed and continued kissing her. It was as if he couldn't get enough of her. In the faint light of the lamp, the only source of light in their room, he explored her body with his eyes. She didn't flinch as she watched him. She was admiring him too: his muscled biceps, his broad shoulders, his well-defined abs.

He took one of her nipples in his mouth like he had done that night in Bohol, and Sarah arched her body against his as explosions of pleasure obliterated her mind. His hand caressed her other breast, his thumb circling her other nipple. She could feel the wetness between her legs as he circled his tongue over her nipple and slowly sucked it. When he heard her moan, he slid his hand between her legs, parting them slightly. He pressed his palm against her wetness, and slowly inserted a finger inside her. Sarah gasped. As he continued caressing her with his fingers, Sarah raised her hips and moaned again. Taking it as a sign, he kissed her all the way down. She couldn't believe what he was about to do. He put his hands under her thighs and pushed them up so that her knees were propped up. All she could see was the top of his head and then she cried out. His tongue was inside her doing all sorts of things that were driving her out of her mind.

'Don't stop!' she cried out. She couldn't help herself. The pleasure built up until she came, wave after wave.

As she relaxed, he moved upwards, over her. He kissed her. It was weird to taste and smell herself on his mouth. But it really turned Sarah on. She felt him hard against her. And then, he slowly entered her. She could see his face darken with desire. He controlled himself so that he was doing it inch by slow inch. And then he quickened his pace. Sarah pushed herself against him, and the incredible feeling of him inside of her made her moan louder with pleasure. He thrust himself harder and faster against her until he shuddered and groaned. 'Sarah,' he said as he pushed himself one last time inside her and they were both spent.

They were cuddled against each other in bed.

'So, we're together?' Sarah asked as she turned to face Benito.

'If this isn't together, I don't know what is.'

'You know, Pete and I never did this.'

'What?' Benito was so shocked he sat up in bed, 'you were together six years.'

'Is there something wrong with that?'

'No. It's just, you know, guys and girls who are in love tend to do this.'

'I know, Benito, I'm not that naïve.'

'Was Pete okay with it?'

'Obviously not. I guess it was why he went out and cheated on me.'

'It still wasn't the right thing to do.'

'I know. But it's still one of the reasons he went looking around.'

'So, you mean, this is your first time?' Benito had a look of wonder.

'Technically, yes.'

'Was this too fast?' Benito looked concerned, all of a sudden. Sarah laughed.

'This was different. Before, I just wanted to control everything. I figured, if I was holding all the cards, I wouldn't make mistakes . . . like my mom. Don't get me wrong. I loved Pete, but I wasn't ready.'

'And now you are?'

'The funny thing is, there really *is* no "ready". This was all fireworks and craziness.'

'How do you feel about this? Do you think you made a mistake?'

She looked into Benito's eyes. He looked worried. It made her heart melt.

'No,' she said, 'I'm happy it was you. I'm happy that I went with the flow.'

'I love you, Sarah,' Benito said. Again, his face was serious. No trace of wisecracking Benito.

'You're *in* love,' Sarah said, 'and I'm in love with you, too, Benito.'

'Is there a difference?'

'For me, love is my mom staying up late at night making the budget work so that Miguel and I don't have to worry. It's her swallowing her pride every time she gets an allowance from my father, so we have food on the table. We're not there,' Sarah said. She felt herself tearing up. She realized that she didn't appreciate her mom half as much as she should.

'Not yet,' Benito said as he touched her cheek.

'And I didn't say we wouldn't get there eventually.'

'So, when you said fireworks and craziness, what did you mean?'

'Are you fishing, Benito Sebastian?'

'Of course, I am.'

Sarah laughed as Benito pulled her closer for a kiss and more . . .

CHAPTER 21

The morning sunlight streamed through the linen curtains, kissing Sarah's face with gentle warmth. As she stirred, she realized that Benito wasn't beside her. He was sitting at the balcony that provided an unfiltered view of Camiguin's lush greenery and shimmering blue sea.

'Morning, sleepyhead,' Benito greeted, his eyes dancing. He handed her a cup of freshly brewed local coffee.

'Morning,' she replied, taking a sip, and letting the rich aroma and taste envelop her senses. He knew just how she liked it, with a little muscovado sugar and a splash of fresh milk.

Their comfort around each other had grown exponentially. Friends first, lovers now—each role seamlessly adding layers to their relationship.

After a quick breakfast they had a kilo of lanzones, straight from the market, to share between the two of them. The fruit, sweet and succulent, was a special kind of indulgence, the result of the island's volcanic soil.

After that, they decided to explore the island some more. This time, Benito was in charge of the itinerary.

'First stop, Old Guiob Church Ruins,' Benito announced, steering their rented scooter through the meandering roads framed by tall palm trees.

The Guiob Church ruins were eerie yet beautiful. Giant acacia trees stood as sentinels around the remnants of the sixteenth-century Spanish church, their roots entwined around the sides of the rectangular-shaped ruins. The walls were thick with moss and foliage, nature reclaiming its space. The eruption of Mt Vulcan in 1871 brought this architectural marvel to its skeletal state.

'It's beautiful,' Sarah whispered in awe. 'These trees are massive.' Sarah stood near the roots of a huge acacia and looked up. The trees' tops joined together above the ruins to create a dense canopy. She snapped some pictures to capture the natural roof they made over the remaining structure of the church.

Benito told her to stop where she was, documenting just how massive the acacia tree was. 'Spread your arms,' Benito said. Her fingertips didn't even reach either side of the massive tree's trunk.

'Check this out,' Benito called. He was standing near one wall covered with thick moss. 'Coral fossils.'

Sarah walked over to where he was and marvelled at the beauty of the church walls. They were made from coral stones. Benito ran his hand along the time-worn stones, remarking, 'It's incredible how something can be broken and beautiful all at once, isn't it?'

Sarah nodded, her response a whisper, 'Just like life—all of us finding beauty in the cracks.'

As they left the church ruins, they were silent in acknowledgement that some moments were too vast to be contained within a camera's frame. They existed in a look, a touch, a shared breath—ephemeral, yet eternal in their hearts.

Next on the itinerary was the Sunken Cemetery, an eerily magnificent spot. A large white cross, standing in the middle of the sea, marked the site where a community had been buried underwater due to the same Mt Vulcan that had laid waste to the Old Guiob Church.

The sea was a deep blue, its waves reflecting the sky above, and the cross stood tall, a sentry watching over history, love, loss, and hope. It was a serene moment; both of them were lost in thought. Sarah felt the urge to capture the moment but refrained. Instead, she rested her head on Benito's shoulder, savouring the weight of the moment in her heart.

The Sunken Cemetery spread before Sarah and Benito, a submerged mystery resting beneath the gentle swells of the sea. They hired a guide, Caloy, to help them navigate the waters. He told them it would be a fifty-metre swim through shallow waters to get to the giant cross and the underwater cemetery. They donned their snorkelling gear and plunged into the sea.

Benito, with his underwater camera ready, gave Sarah a reassuring nod.

Through the diffused sunlight, the remnants of the old graves marked by multiple stone crosses were a ghostly vision, adorned now with vibrant corals and anemones. Schools of fish darted between the cracks and crevices, and for a moment, Sarah felt the weight of history beneath her.

Benito captured the silent ballet of marine life weaving through the tombstones, his camera a silent observer of the underwater landscape unfolding before them. Every snapshot was a tribute, a moment frozen in time, just as the memories of those who rested there were held in the silent keep of the ocean.

Caloy pointed out a particularly large brain coral, nestled atop what might have once been the cornerstone of a family crypt.

Sarah watched as a solitary clownfish emerged from the folds of a sea anemone, its vibrant stripes stark against the muted colours of the stone. It struck her then, how life found a way, even in the remnants of loss and devastation.

Their dive was a silent communion, a shared experience that transcended words. When they finally surfaced, the afternoon sun made the water sparkle.

Benito reviewed the images on his camera, each one a story in itself, capturing the serene beauty of the underwater cemetery.

As they left the waterside, Sarah felt a new-found appreciation for the resilience of memory and the way nature could reclaim any space, just like the church ruins that they visited earlier. The Sunken Cemetery was a symbol of how a place of death and destruction could once again be teeming with life.

Their next adventure was waiting, the Giant Clam Sanctuary, another memory to share between them. The sanctuary was nestled in the quiet Kibila Beach, a vibrant testament to the island's commitment to marine conservation.

The air was filled with the scent of salt and earth, mingling together as a reminder of the island's volcanic fertility that fed into the richness of the marine life here.

Their guide, Boyet, was a local teenager. They were surprised at his passion for explaining everything about the clams, just like a marine biologist would. He showed them the huge concrete tanks where certain clams grew. The tanks allowed them to reproduce before they were moved out into the coral reef off the shore.

He told them that the entire sanctuary started as a family-run business to protect the few remaining giant clams in the water. All the guides and staff members were from the nearby Cantaan area.

The concrete tanks were used to grow pearl-producing clams as well as nurturing giant clams, and the sanctuary was created not only to protect the giant clams, but also to provide various income streams, from tourism to pearl farming, for the local villages. He told them that the ocean nursery was home to hundreds of individual giant clams of various sizes that were protected and nurtured in the sheltered waters around the bay. 'The clams are more than just shells,' he explained, his eyes alight with admiration. 'They are essential to the coral reef's health, and each one can live up to a century or more.'

Boyet further explained that the giant clams were bottom dwellers just like starfish, urchins, and crabs. Algae lived in their tissues and shells. The algae photosynthesized and the Giant Clams consumed the by-products of the photosynthesis to grow themselves and to achieve their huge size.

'How huge?' they asked Boyet.

Apparently, they could grow to almost five feet in length and weigh up to 500 kilograms. Both Benito and Sarah were amazed by all the facts that Boyet shared with ease.

They strapped on their masks and snorkels and were taken out into the open ocean by Boyet.

The water there was shallow and sandy, and the clams that were growing on the sporadic coral and seabed were small and young. Boyet told them as they bobbed up that the clams in the area were no more than six months old. However, many of them could live for another hundred years, some even longer.

They were excited as they got their first glimpse of the giant clams. The colourful clams shrank and expanded, in and out of the opening of their shells, as Sarah and Benito moved along the neat rows admiring the strange creatures. Their vibrant mantles were a kaleidoscope of iridescent blues, greens, and purples. Each clam seemed like an underwater treasure, a living gemstone half-buried in the ocean's embrace. Benito captured the essence of their magnificence with his underwater camera.

As Sarah floated above a clam with a mantle as blue as the sky above, she reached out with a finger, careful not to touch it, respecting the delicate balance of this ecosystem.

The sanctuary seemed to suspend time. But as the sun signalled the passing of the afternoon, they knew they had to leave the underwater Garden of Eden.

'Camiguin is a gem,' Sarah said to Benito as they floated side by side, admiring a luminescent coral. Benito caught her hand and gave it a gentle squeeze. Their eyes met, and even in the refracted light, the message was clear: They were falling deeper in love with each passing moment.

Climbing out of the water, they thanked Boyet, their minds a swirl of colours and shapes from the sanctuary's depths. On the sandy shore, they shared a quiet moment, appreciating what they had just experienced.

Back at their cozy resort, nestled amidst tropical vegetation, they started to pack. Sarah neatly folded her clothes and set aside her essentials, pausing as she saw the camera lying on the bed.

'You know,' Sarah reflected, 'cameras are great, but the best moments are already captured here,' she added, placing her hand over her heart.

Benito came over and embraced her. 'Are you ready for the next chapter? Seven Falls in South Cotabato, here we come,' he joked. Sarah looked at him and smiled. 'With you, I think I'll always be ready.'

'We better rest up. It's going to be busy tomorrow.'

'Yes, but tonight, we dream of clams and hot springs,' Sarah replied with a smile, turning to give him a gentle kiss.

As they curled up together, the memories of the day were like a series of snapshots laid out in their minds, a montage of moments that, while not all captured on camera, were deeply etched in their shared journey.

Sarah knew that the most beautiful moments with Benito were the ones stored in the depths of her heart.

The next morning, Sarah took a peek at her blog and social media pages. It had been a while since she had last checked it.

She sat up, heart quickening with a mixture of hope and anxiety. The digital world, it seemed, had not been silent in the last few days.

Her blog had become a small beacon, drawing in readers from across the globe. Comments were pouring in, a mix of awestruck responses and heartfelt thanks from those who had been longing to see and feel such natural wonders but had never had the chance.

Her Instagram was alive with activity; followers were captivated by the vibrant images of Kawasan Falls. Each photograph she had taken and shared was now a conduit, connecting her experience to the emotions and imaginations of others. Her Facebook page was no different, with shares and likes accumulating faster than she could keep track.

As the numbers grew, so did a subtle pressure in the back of Sarah's mind. She had hoped for an audience, but now that she had one, the reality was daunting. Each follower was a person looking forward to her posts, eager for more. She felt a weight of expectation to keep the content coming, to make each entry as engaging and vivid as the last.

She spent the early morning replying to comments, engaging with her new-found community. Their words were encouraging, each message and share fuelling her commitment to her blog and her journey. Still, the task was time-consuming, and she realized that balancing her online presence with her travels would be a challenge.

Later in the morning, the initial wave of messages had slowed, and Sarah took a moment to reflect. The pressure was real, but it was not a burden. It was motivation. Her audience was not a faceless mass but a group of individuals who shared her passion and appreciated her efforts.

With renewed determination, Sarah began to plan her future posts, her future travels. She could explore local sites, delve into the history of the waterfalls she had visited, or share tips for would-be travellers.

The excitement was back, tingling through her veins. *Sarah, the Seeker* was more than a blog or a social media account. It was a journey, her journey, and it was just beginning. She would share her passion with the world, one waterfall at a time.

Sarah's fingers were once again poised over the keyboard. The blog was her gateway to the world, and she was ready to embrace whatever came next. She smiled to herself. The digital world was no longer a foreign place but an extension of her very quest.

'Ready to go?' Benito asked.

'Ready as ever,' Sarah smiled back.

CHAPTER 22

'Omigod!' Anya screamed into Sarah's ear over the phone. It was like a repeat of Bohol except, this time, she was screaming with happiness. 'My two best friends!' she said, threatening the state of Sarah's eardrums.

'Anya, my ears,' Sarah said. But she smiled.

'Okay, okay,' Anya said, calming down, 'Can I talk to Benito?'

Sarah called Benito over and gave him her phone, 'Anya,' she said, indicating the phone. She left the two of them to catch up.

Sarah and Benito were on the deck of a ferry on the way to Cagayan de Oro. It would take them two hours, but Sarah was sure the time would pass quickly especially because she was with Benito. Benito mentioned that his cousin, Joey, would meet them at the Macabalan Port in Cagayan de Oro.

Benito handed back the phone to her with a look of amusement on his face.

'Have you told your mom?' Anya asked Sarah.

'Not yet. I thought you, of all people, should know first.'

'I'm so happy for both of you. It's about time.'

'What do you mean by it's about time? What do you know that you haven't told me before?'

'It doesn't matter now!' Anya laughed into the phone.

'No, seriously, Anya.'

She heard Anya sigh.

'All I know is that Benito's been waiting a long time.'

'That's what he told me.'

'Well, it's true.'

'You never mentioned this.'

'He told me not to.'

Sarah called her mom. She was grateful that her mom wasn't into hysterics, like Anya, but she was happy, nevertheless. She knew that her mom always had a soft spot for Benito.

'Sarah, when you come back, I have to talk to you about something.'

'Ma, why can't you just tell me now?'

'Because you're on vacation! It can wait.'

'Okay.'

'I'm glad Benito's there with you. I really like that boy. Stay safe, okay?'

'We will. Love you.'

Sarah wondered, briefly, about what her mom had said, but she soon shrugged it off and walked back to Benito.

'Kumusta ka, bai?' greeted the tall guy in shades and a plain blue cotton T-shirt. Sarah could tell that he and Benito had the same good-looking gene running through their family tree. They exchanged greetings in Bisaya as Sarah stood there wishing she had learned more Bisaya before leaving. She had Benito to consult now.

'Manong Joey, akong girlfriend, Sarah,' he said. Did she hear 'girlfriend'? Benito couldn't wait. It sounded funny, but, yes, it was true! He shook her hand and leaned in for a beso.

'Glad to meet you, Sarah!' Sarah was surprised by how warmly he greeted her.

'Likewise!'

'So, Manong, you sure that taking the bus is the best route?'

'Yup. I'll drive you to the terminal. I've already called up Carmela. You're staying at her place near the T'boli School of Indigenous Knowledge and Traditions.'

'That's great! Sarah, here, is really determined to get to Lake Sebu. Nothing can stop her.'

'Lake Sebu is really beautiful. But you have to hurry. It takes eight hours to get to General Santos and another hour to get to Marbel. From Marbel, you'll spend another forty-five minutes to an hour to get to Surrallah. From there, it's best if you just take the van from the Integrated Transport Terminal to Lake Sebu. That's another forty-five minutes. You have a long day ahead of you.'

It was a good thing they took the earliest ferry ride to Cagayan de Oro.

The trip to Lake Sebu was, indeed, gruelling. Sarah and Benito didn't get much time to talk because they took turns taking naps on the buses and preserving their energy for

their trip to their final set of waterfalls. Sarah was glad for
the company, though. She tried imagining herself travelling
alone from Cagayan de Oro to General Santos City to Marbel
and then to Surrallah. The views, even from the buses, were
magnificent. There were vast plantations of pineapples, corn,
coconut, and bananas as far as the eye could see. Behind
them were the rolling hills of Bukidnon. They were verdant
in the foreground, but purple and blue closer to the horizon.
But she didn't speak a word of Bisaya and she didn't have
Benito's easy-going, unfazed know-how on travelling. He
was like a human compass. He could tell where north, south,
west, and east were. Sarah could tell where her left and
where her right was, but that was it. As she leaned her head
on Benito's shoulder, she felt that she couldn't have been
happier or luckier to be with him on the way to Lake Sebu.

The van driver knew exactly where to take them when they
said they were looking for Carmel Eko of the TSIKAT
school. Their enterprising driver, Waning, gave them his
phone number, which they gladly took down, when they told
him that they had plans of visiting Seven Falls.

'Sir, take the zip line. It's the best way to see all the falls.
I can drive you there.'

Carmel was the most gracious host. She had long black
hair that she tied back and away from her high forehead.
She was dressed in traditional T'boli k'gal dress of woven
cloth and she also wore colourful, traditional nomong bead
earrings that cascaded from her ears.

'Your cousin, Joey Neri, called me,' Carmel said in a soft
voice. They introduced themselves to her.

'Manong Joey says that the best place to stay is at your house near the school.'

'Yes, it's comfortable but you won't get any luxuries there.'

'We really appreciate that you accommodated us, Ms Carmel. I'm happy to be nearby your school. I would love to sit and learn too,' Sarah said.

'I'm very glad that you're here to learn, Sarah. We should talk some more.'

'Ms Carmel, for the rest of the afternoon, we plan to visit Seven Falls and maybe hike to one of the falls. We can spend the day, tomorrow, at the school,' Benito said.

'Just call me Carmel,' she said and smiled. 'All right. I'll take you to the house so you can settle down. Enjoy your trip to the falls. My nephew, Doy, can take you on a boat ride early tomorrow morning and then you can go to the school.'

They put their stuff down at a communal cottage made mostly of bamboo and got ready for their afternoon at the falls.

They got in touch with Waning who picked them up in his habal-habal, the best transport to the falls. It didn't take them long to get to the eco-tourism park. As soon as they got there, they were encouraged to walk to the first two falls, Hikong Alo and Hikong Bente, as they were just a short hike away from the zip line ride. Since it wasn't a busy day at the park (it was a weekday), one of the guides at the park walked with them down to Hikong Alo and the 774-step trail to Hikong Bente.

He explained to them that each of the waterfalls had a name: Hikong Alo (Passage falls), Hikong Bente (Immeasurable falls), Hikong B'lebed (Zigzag or coil falls), Hikong Lowig (Booth falls), Hikong K'Fo-I (Wildflower falls), Hikong Ukol (Short falls), and Hikong Tonok (Soil falls). The zip line had two legs. The first one would give them a beautiful view of the most majestic of the falls, Hikong Bente. It would take roughly 45 seconds only. The second leg of the zip line would give them a view of Hikong B'lebed, Hikong Lowig, and Hikong K'Fo-I, three interconnected falls cascading from one to the other.

Sarah was excited to hear the familiar sound of waterfalls in the distance. It was music to her ears. Benito took her hand in his and they followed their guide to Hikong Alo. It stood 35 feet above ground and the basin was misty with water spray. Benito squeezed her hand. It was truly majestic. All they could do was stare. The cascade was silky smooth and the water at its basin was a deep emerald. They asked their guide if they could swim but he discouraged it because of the strong water current. He did tell them to dip their feet, which both Benito and Sarah did. They sat side by side as they cooled their feet at the bank of the basin. Sarah took a small stone and put it in her backpack. It was a deep greenish brown.

'What's that?' Benito asked.

'Oh, nothing, a small souvenir. I've taken a small pebble from each of the waterfalls I've visited, and I keep them.'

'So, this is your seventh?'

'Yup.'

'What are you going to do with them?'

'I don't know. I haven't thought it through. Put them in a bottle maybe? I've written down what I've learned from each of the waterfalls in my journal.'

'You are the most organized obsessive compulsive person I know. I mean, it's enough that you've been on this adventure. But you actually wrote down what you've learned. You should have a blog like Marley.'

'Actually, I already have one,' Sarah smiled.

'So, what have you learned?'

'A lot! I think of each of the waterfalls as a mentor.'

'That's insightful, Sarah.'

'Each of them has a personality, I think. They're like my seven muses.'

'Technically, more than seven.'

'Technically. But you get what I mean.'

'Yeah. Look at this one. It's absolutely exquisite. What did she teach you?'

'She!' Sarah laughed. 'You know, you're right. This one feels like a she, just like Batlag and Kinabuan Falls.' Sarah closed her eyes for a moment.

'This one,' Sarah continued, 'this one teaches me to go with the flow. Just chill.'

'I dig that.'

They proceeded to Hikong Bente. The downward walk was easy. Sarah knew that coming up would be a challenge. She remembered the uphill climb back to Marilaque Highway after their visit to Kinabuan Falls. Well, they had the whole afternoon, anyway.

If Hikong Alo was graceful and smooth, Hikong Bente was tall and powerful, like a warrior. Hikong Bente stood

70 feet above ground, the tallest of all the seven falls. They took pictures at the viewing deck and moved closer to get a better look.

Up close, Sarah held her breath when she saw the rainbows that formed over the mists at the base of Hikong Bente. It wasn't just the waterfall that was beautiful, it was standing in the middle of a lush forest with a river cutting through it. Sarah couldn't wait to get near the riverbank.

Sarah and Benito did the same thing at Hikong Alo, they took off their hiking sandals and waded into the water at the riverbank. The water was cold, but they didn't mind. They got treated to an up-close-and-personal look at the huge waterfall. It was just awe-inspiring. Benito picked up a pebble from where they stood. It was small and looked oddly heart-shaped.

'This is for you,' he said, handing the pebble to her. It was light brown with streaks of grey. Sarah took it in her hand and put it in her pocket.

'This one's special,' Sarah said, taking Benito's hand.

'Really? What did you learn from this one?' They both looked out at Hikong Bente.

'Listen when you're being called.'

'That's beautiful.' Benito said. 'I'm sorry for even suggesting that we skip this part of your trip.' Sarah squeezed his hand in response and kissed him.

Sarah was excited about the zip line, but she was also a bit scared. It would be her first time riding one. Actually, she realized, her entire trip was a series of firsts. There was no other way but to go all in.

They opted for the double zip line (two people at a time). Sarah's heart was beating fast while she stepped into the harness. They were fitted out with helmets and gloves. Then, they got onto the platform where the cables were located. Both she and Benito were parallel and in horizonal 'Superman' flying positions. The platform staff took their photos and then stashed all their gadgets back into their backpacks. When Sarah heard the carabiners clicking into place, she took a deep breath. No turning back any more. She heard the head of the crew give the go signal.

All of a sudden, Sarah was flying in the air! As she was instructed, she looked to the right. She was rewarded with a great top view of Hikong Bente. Sarah was awestruck at the rainbows forming above the basin once again. The rest of the area around it was deep green forest. The length of the ride measured 740 metres. It only took a few seconds, but it was epic. Everything seemed to be happening in slow motion.

They landed on the first station successfully. Instead of fear, Sarah only felt excitement this time. She felt fully alive. Now, it was time for their second leg. After the lift-off, she turned left to see the cascading Hikong B'lebed, Hikong Lowig, and Hikong K'Fo-I. From afar, all three of them looked like one big waterfall but Sarah noticed how Hikong B'lebed's basin flowed to form Hikong Lowig. From Hikong Lowig, the water curved and formed Hikong K'Fo-I. Again, it was just a few seconds. The entire length was shorter than the first leg at 400 metres, but it felt like the ride of a lifetime. She had just conquered one of the most intimidating series of zip lines in the Philippines, maybe even Asia. She felt proud of herself.

They had a hell of a time climbing back up towards the eco-park, but they made it. And it was all worth it.

Journal entry
Seventh Stop: Seven Falls

Seven Falls in South Cotabato was an absolute marvel with its seven different waterfalls, one following the other. The highlight was taking a zip line ride that soared over five of these waterfalls. The experience was exhilarating, to say the least. Chasing after waterfalls requires a bit of a fitness regime. Waterfalls usually require trekking and going up and down stairs or barely carved-out niches. Watch for my blog on the basics of adventure fitness.

Here I had an up-close encounter with two of the seven falls.

Hikong Alo
Deep greenish brown.
Go with the flow. Just chill.

Hikong Bente
Light-brown pebble, heart-shaped with streaks of grey.
Listen when you're being called.

CHAPTER 23

Sarah woke up to the sound of a haunting flute melody. Even though their bodies ached from their trek and zip line ride the day before, Sarah and Benito still woke up early for their scheduled boat ride in Lake Sebu with Doy as their guide. They had slept communal-style at the T'boli house of Carmel. Sarah was glad for the bucket-flush toilet in their cottage. Carmel was right, it was not luxurious, but everything was clean and very comfortable.

Doy patiently waited for them outside their bamboo cottage. After greeting them, he led them to another house where he asked permission to use the wooden boat. The house wasn't very far from the bank of Lake Sebu. Doy and Benito dragged the boat towards the lake and, pretty soon, they were paddling the serene lake in the early morning mist.

Sarah took in the beautiful pink water lilies that lined the lake, still closed but already starting to bloom. The lake itself was a perfect mirror to the sky and the surrounding mountains and trees. She was in awe of Lake Sebu.

After their scenic boat ride, Doy led them back to the TSIKAT where Carmel was already waiting for them.

'We put up this school because we wanted to preserve the local culture,' Carmel said, taking Sarah's arm. T'boli children swarmed around them as they entered the main building. Like the cottage where they stayed, the main material of the building was bamboo. There were other surrounding cottages, but they were higher, propped up on stilts.

'I'm glad you're here not as a typical tourist, Sarah,' Carmel said. 'Not many people want to hear the sad story of our people.'

'Sad story, Carmel?'

'There are only two million of us left, the indigenous tribes here in Mindanao: Kalagan, Ubo, Manobo, B'laan, Maguindanao Muslims and our tribe, the T'boli. If it weren't for the support of some families who see the value of our heritage, we would be wiped out of here. Our people hunted and foraged these lands for centuries. But we're losing our land. We can't live the way we used to.'

'That's terrible, Carmel. What can we do?' Sarah could see the sadness in Carmel's eyes. She couldn't just stand there, listening to her, without doing anything.

'The most we can do now is preserve some of our traditions and rely on tourism.'

'Is that enough?'

'I'm not sure.'

They entered one of the schoolrooms where children were being taught to play the sloli, the traditional T'boli bamboo flute. It reminded Sarah of the flute music she'd heard when she woke up that morning. It was a haunting melody. As she listened, Sarah realized that the sound that was coming from the flute was a thousand years old. *We can't lose this*, she thought to herself.

They listened to a few more performances: hegelung, a string guitar, and the kulintang, a series of brass gongs.

'Come,' Carmel said to Sarah and Benito, 'the children will be eating their lunch.' They followed Carmel to the classroom where the children lined up with porcelain plates and recycled plastic ice cream tubs to get their serving of rice, tilapia fish, and vegetables.

'We rely on the American Women's Club in Manila for our children's lunch,' Carmel explained, 'Many of our children are undernourished. Our families hardly hunt or forage any more. We have farms but the weather has changed. We can't rely on our old ways. I don't mean to sound depressing. But that's just how it is.'

Sarah pulled Benito aside.

'I feel terrible. Benito, we've been to some of the most beautiful places in the Philippines but I'm afraid that these will get exploited, or worse, they'll get degraded by climate change.'

Benito was silent. He put his arm around her and squeezed her hand.

'Well, we don't need to have an answer right now, right?'

'You're right.'

Sarah thought about her recent retrenchment and how it paled in comparison to what the T'boli tribe was going through. It was her biggest tragedy so far. But what was it compared to the situation that the T'bolis faced?

They joined Carmel again. She was engaged in a lively discussion with the kids and the teachers. Carmel gave Sarah and Benito the same simple meal that everyone was having. Among all their food trips along the way, Sarah felt that this was the most meaningful one because it was shared with the people of the community they were visiting.

In the afternoon, Carmel said they could watch the dream weavers at work.

'Why are they called dream weavers, Carmel?'

'This is an ancient tradition. They believe that the designs for the cloth were passed on to them through their dreams, their ancestors' dreams, and all granted through the Fu Dalu, the spirit of the abaca itself. It's a sacred activity.'

Sarah and Benito sat by as they watched an old master weaver show a younger weaver the ropes. It looked like a very taxing physical activity, requiring the rigorous pulling and pushing of the backstrap loom or legogong.

'It takes months to produce a bolt of cloth,' Carmel said. 'We're really sad that we lost Lang Dulay, the famed master weaver of the T'boli. She passed away in 2015,' Carmel continued, 'But we're making sure that her legacy doesn't go away.'

It was easy to see why it took months to produce. Everything was done by hand. And they didn't see the dyeing process, but they were told it was all done by hand too.

'Where can we buy the T'nalak?'

'We can go there later, at the Princess House Store.'

After their tour of the cottages where different grades were being taught subjects in their native language, they proceeded to Gono Kem Bo-I, the Princess House Store.

'This is the Cooperative of Women in Health and Development,' Carmel said as they approached the nipa hut, 'The design of this house is after the Gono Kem Bo-I or T'boli Princess House. 'They sell T'nalak, embroidered items, beads, and brass jewellery. Go ahead and take a look inside.'

Sarah was fascinated with the black, red, and natural abaca colours of the T'nalak. She immediately got herself a bolt of cloth. She was sure her mom would love it. She got

Miguel a brass bell in the shape of a man. She also got beaded bracelets for both Anya and Marley.

'What did you get, Benito?' Sarah asked.

'It's not for me. It's for you,' he presented her with an intricate bracelet with little brass bells attached to it.

'You shouldn't have!' Sarah said but he was already putting it around her left wrist. 'It's exquisite, Benito. Thank you!'

As they headed back to the cottage where Sarah and Benito were staying, Sarah thanked Carmel profusely.

'I learned so much today, Carmel. Not enough, though.'

'Some people are content to be tourists—they'll ride the zip line over the waterfalls, enjoy the view, and go back without ever knowing about the T'boli. Thank you for taking the time to visit the school and to understand what we're doing here.'

'I wish there was more that I could do.'

'Being aware is a good start,' Carmel smiled. 'You can tell other people.'

'That's what I'll do, Carmel. I promise.'

'Get a good night's rest. You have a long day of travel tomorrow.'

Before turning in for bed, Sarah checked her phone for messages.

She had one from an unknown number. *Hi, Sarah! This is Jilian from Ascentra Connect. I tried calling you around two weeks ago. We were impressed with your CV. We'd like to invite you for an interview for an Account Manager role. When are you free this week to get on a call?*

Sarah's heart leapt to her throat. It felt like a lifetime ago when she was sending out her résumé. What was she going to do now?

Sarah: *Hi, Jilian! Nice to e-meet you. I'm travelling right now. The signal isn't so great here in South Cotabato. Can I get back to you by tomorrow regarding the schedule?*

Jilian: *Thanks for replying, Sarah! No worries at all. Looking forward to hearing from you.*

CHAPTER 24

Sarah and Benito decided to spend another day in Cotabato before heading off to Cagayan de Oro and then back to Manila. They left their luggage at Lake Sebu, making plans to return for it before heading off to their next destination. Their first stop was Lake Holon. The lake was cradled by the ancient Mt Parker, or Mt Melibengoy in T'boli. They decided to skip the usual stations and go straight to the lake. They rode a habal-habal with their guide, Roding. He told them that the lake was named after an American who accompanied General Parker. They both died in a plane crash during the 1930s when they were surveying the place. Thus, the names Mt Parker and Lake Holon.

As early morning painted the sky in pastel hues, Sarah and Benito arrived at the lake, a serene gem. It shimmered under the morning light, its crystal-clear waters reflecting the sky above. They trekked through lush forests, the path unveiling the lake's stunning beauty bit by bit. The air was fresh, the scent of trees and earth mingling together.

Upon reaching the lake's edge, they were greeted by its tranquil waters and the symphony of nature around them. The calmness of the lake, with its turquoise embrace, offered a perfect setting for reflection and heartfelt conversations.

'This place is incredible,' Sarah whispered, not wanting to disturb the tranquillity around them.

'It is, isn't it?' Benito replied, his eyes mirroring her wonder.

'So, tell me about Samantha,' Sarah began, her gaze fixed on the lake.

'Why do you want to talk about my ex?'

'I'm curious.'

Benito looked at her, perhaps sensing the seriousness of the question. 'Fair enough. I have nothing to hide about my relationships. Samantha was warm, compassionate, and smart. We connected on many levels, but we were just fresh out of high school. I knew our relationship wouldn't last.'

'Because?' Sarah's eyes met his as they walked towards the lakeshore.

'Because we were both still so immature.'

Sarah gave him a look.

'Okay, I take it back. I was too immature for Samantha.'

Sarah smiled and nodded, appreciating Benito's honesty.

It was too cold to take a swim in the lake, so they decided to have breakfast and native coffee at a nearby store.

After that, it was time to head back to Lake Sebu, and then to Surallah.

They made sure to visit the Surallah Tri-People Monument. The monument, a symbol of unity and cultural harmony, stood proudly in the heart of Surallah, a testament to the coexistence of the diverse communities in the region. It was an impressive structure, with sculptures representing the indigenous T'boli, Muslim, and Christian settlers, each figure intricately designed to showcase their unique cultural heritage.

As they approached, the sun was high in the sky, casting long shadows over the monument. The area around the monument was a blend of lush greenery and well-maintained landscapes, creating a serene atmosphere that invited quiet contemplation and appreciation of the region's rich cultural history.

'There's a sense of unity and acceptance here that I've rarely felt elsewhere,' Sarah commented. Benito nodded.

'So, what about Eliza?'

Benito smiled. 'Okay, I guess I'm not off the hook yet.' He looked out towards the horizon, his eyes distant. 'Eliza was fiery . . . We had an exciting relationship. We burned brightly, lighting up each other's worlds. But fires like that aren't meant to last. The initial thrill died down. And then, it was all fights.'

Sarah took in his words, the honesty in Benito's voice with the solemn backdrop of the Tri-People Monument.

As the day edged into late afternoon, Sarah and Benito arrived at Plaza Heneral Santos. The plaza, a bustling centre of activity, contrasted starkly with the quiet serenity of their earlier destinations. It was a lively space, filled with the vibrant energy of the city. People from all walks of life mingled in the square, surrounded by historic buildings and modern sculptures that celebrated the rich history and progress of General Santos City.

The setting sun cast a golden glow over the plaza, illuminating the faces of statues and the smiles of passers-by. Street vendors lined the pathways, offering a variety of local delicacies and crafts. The air was filled with the aroma of grilled seafood and the sound of laughter and music, creating an atmosphere of warmth and community. In the middle of it all, Benito excused himself. His dad was calling. Sarah shooed him away and just enjoyed the afternoon sun.

As they walked through the plaza, Sarah finally voiced the question that had been lingering in her mind. 'What about—'

'Gia,' Benito finished for her.

'She must have been quite different from the others.'

Benito nodded, acknowledging the stark contrast. 'Gia was . . . she was like a dream, almost surreal. Her world was all glamour and spotlights. I was in awe of her. She was gorgeous. She seemed to glide through life with such ease.'

'And did you love her?' Sarah's question was direct, her voice tinged with a vulnerability she rarely showed.

Benito took her hand, his touch gentle. 'Gia was incredible, but I wasn't devoted to her. I didn't feel what I've always felt for you. With her, it was more about the allure of her world, a world that I knew deep down wasn't mine.'

Benito squeezed Sarah's hand. 'What's really on your mind, Sarah?'

Sarah searched his eyes, looking for the truth in his words.

'In Camiguin, you said you loved me.'

'And I meant it. I know you explained about being "in love" and "love". But I'm willing to go all in.'

'Can you really be serious, Benito? After all this time and all these past girlfriends in your life?'

Benito's response was firm, his eyes locked on hers. 'I've always been serious about you, Sarah. It may have seemed like I was just playing around. Is that what you think?'

'I thought you were always chasing the next thrill . . .'

'My heart has always known where it belongs.' The sincerity in his voice was undeniable, resonating with the truth of his feelings.

As they sat down on a bench, watching the hustle and bustle of Plaza Heneral Santos, Benito leaned in closer. 'I've been waiting for you, always. And now that I have you here, I don't plan on letting go.'

'I want this to work,' Sarah said. She and Pete hadn't worked out. Her parents' marriage hadn't worked out. 'I'm scared because . . . I love you.' There, she said it. It wasn't easy to say.

'I'm scared too, Sarah. But, I love you more than I'm scared.'

The night unfolded, and in the privacy of their shared space, another hotel room in South Cotabato (this time with just one bed), their connection deepened, affirming Benito's commitment in the most intimate way. A rich collection of experiences behind them and a promise of more to come, they couldn't help but pull each other close. In that secluded space, words became superfluous. Their bodies spoke a language only they understood, every touch a sentence, every look a paragraph. It was a moment of affirmation, of commitment, an intimate contract sealed with heartbeats and breaths.

As they lay together, Benito whispered about a new development. 'My dad wants me to handle some business in Davao. Instead of heading straight to Cagayan de Oro, then Manila, how about we take a side trip to Davao?'

'You know I'm not in a hurry to get home.'

Benito laughed out loud. 'My meeting is in the morning. I'll take care of our itinerary in Davao for the afternoon. You'll love it.'

'How's the mobile signal in Davao City?'

'It's great! Why do you ask?'

'I have to take a call from a recruiter.'

'Wow! That's fantastic news, Sarah! There's Wi-Fi at the hotel, so you won't have any problems.'

Sarah quickly sent out a text message to Jilian asking if a 10.00 a.m. video call for the following day would be okay. She confirmed right away.

As they lay wrapped in each other's arms, Sarah knew the journey—through Cotabato, through their past, through their uncertainties—had been worth it. And so was the wait for each other. It was a realization as expansive and intricate as the locales they had explored, and as deep and nuanced as the love that had finally found its time to bloom. And now, here was opportunity knocking on her door.

CHAPTER 25

They were off to Davao on the first available bus at around 4.45 a.m., hardly catching up on sleep during the four-hour trip. As soon as they reached Davao City, Benito booked them at a hotel so Sarah could catch up on sleep.

Sarah woke up to the smell of coffee.

'What's that wonderful smell?'

'Hey, sleep in if you need to,' Benito said gently.

'I'm feeling refreshed. Besides, I have a 10.00 a.m. call.'

'Right! Good luck with the interview. You'll ace it.'

Benito brought her a cup in bed.

'This is Arabica coffee cultivated in Mt Apo. It's the best.'

Sarah took a sip and closed her eyes. It tasted just right, with a hint of fruitiness. The aftertaste was smooth, with none of the bitterness of a regular cup.

'It *is* the best,' Sarah agreed.

'I have a surprise for you.' Benito smiled. 'After all my work is done for the day, we're off to Samal Island this afternoon.'

'Is it far?' Sarah was well-rested, but she wasn't up for another trek like the ones they had in South Cotabato.

'Nope. It'll just take an hour, maximum. But that's not the best part.'

'What's the best part?'

'We're going to Hagimit Falls.'

'Oh my goodness!' Sarah exclaimed. The best surprise, indeed. 'A bonus waterfall!'

'We can take it easy and spend the whole afternoon there. Also, it's a weekday. We'll have it all to ourselves.'

'Woohoo!'

'When I get back from my meeting, let's have lunch at the restaurant downstairs. It's another surprise.'

'You're spoiling me!'

With a kiss on her forehead, Benito was off to his meeting.

Sarah chose her best, wrinkle-free travel blouse in navy and put on some work-appropriate make-up. Before the call, Sarah closed her eyes and took a deep breath. *Universe, is this a sign?* She was feeling so many feelings. She was a little nervous. It was her first work interview in years. She was a little excited. They were *impressed* with her résumé. She was also conflicted. She'd imagined a whole other life on this trip. She wasn't one to close doors, though, so Sarah clicked on the 'Join' button on the calendar invite from Jilian.

The girl on the screen reminded her of her old self, confident smile, neatly swept-up hair, white collared blouse, crisp black blazer.

'Hi, Sarah! Nice to finally see your face. I'm Jilian from Ascentra Connect. We're a leading business process outsourcing company. Have you heard of us before?'

'Hi, Jilian! Yes, I have. Nice to see you too.'

'Great! I'm glad to hear that, Sarah. As you may know, Ascentra Connect prides itself on delivering top-tier services to our clients, and we believe this is only possible through the talents and dedication of our team members. Given your impressive background and skills, you seem like you could be a fantastic fit here. Could you start by telling me about a particularly challenging situation you faced in your previous role and how you managed it?'

Wow, Sarah thought, *she's gone straight for the challenging situation and skipped the tell-me-about-yourself part.* Sarah nodded thoughtfully before responding. 'Sure, Jilian. One of the most challenging experiences I encountered was being retrenched due to an account closing. It was unexpected, and initially, it shook my confidence. But I took it as an opportunity to reflect on my career path and focus on personal growth. I used the time to focus on my health goals and some online training. This period also taught me resilience and the importance of adaptability in the face of change.'

Jilian listened attentively, leaning forward. 'Sarah, thank you for being so open about that experience. Retrenchment is indeed a tough challenge, but it's clear you've approached it with a positive and proactive mindset. Your ability to turn a difficult situation into an opportunity for growth speaks volumes about your character and professional resilience. I want you to know that here at Ascentra Connect, we value the journey and the learnings as much as the achievements. Retrenchment doesn't diminish your qualifications or the impressive accomplishments you've achieved.'

Sarah smiled, appreciating Jilian's empathetic response. 'Thank you for understanding, Jilian. I believe every experience shapes us, and I'm excited about the prospect of bringing my skills and learnings to Ascentra Connect.'

'Can you tell me more about yourself?' Jilian asked, 'What are you like outside of the office?'

'I'm actually in the middle of an adventure,' Sarah said with a smile, 'I'm on a quest to visit seven waterfalls in the country. It was a spontaneous decision, driven by my love for nature and my desire to challenge myself physically and mentally. It's been amazing. It reminds me of the importance of staying curious, embracing new experiences, and continually learning, values I bring to my professional life as well.'

Jilian's eyes lit up with interest. 'That sounds like an incredible adventure, Sarah! Your willingness to learn and step out of your comfort zone isn't limited to your professional life. Those are exactly the kind of qualities we appreciate and encourage at Ascentra Connect. It seems you're not just fit for the role, but also for our company culture. Let's dive into specifics about how your skills and experiences can contribute to our ongoing projects and team dynamics.'

They talked a little bit more about the job specifics, but it was clear to Sarah that Jilian was engaged and interested.

'I'll be recommending you for the next round of interviews, Sarah,' Jilian said. 'What's your schedule like? When will you be done with your trip?'

'I'm on my last leg. I should be back in Manila by next week.'

'Great. I'll get in touch with you next week.'

Sarah called up her mom to share the good news.

'Ma! I got a call from Ascentra Connect, one of the BPOs I applied to!'

'That's wonderful, anak! How's your trip? Won't you come home soon?'

'Sorry, Ma. We got a bit delayed. We're here in Davao now because Benito's dad asked him to take care of some business.'

'Okay, Sarah. Someone wants to talk to you.' She could hear her pass on the phone.

'Ate! I miss you!'

Sarah couldn't help but smile. She wanted to hug Miguel over the phone. 'I miss you too, Miguel. I'll be home soon.'

'I can't wait. I heard from Ma that Kuya Benito is your boyfriend now. Uuuuy!' Miguel teased.

Sarah laughed. 'Stop teasing or I won't bring home your pasalubong.'

'You have pasalubong? Yay! Hurry home, okay?'

'I will!'

CHAPTER 26

Lunch was at the hotel's restaurant that overlooked the hotel pool. When their lunch spread arrived, Sarah was caught off guard.

'Benito, this looks extra special!' Sarah exclaimed. A huge piece of grilled tuna jowl was laid out before them.

'We missed the tuna auction at Gen San, but I didn't want you to miss out on tuna panga. It's really awesome.'

Benito wasn't kidding about how awesome it would taste. The tuna panga had a distinct, robust flavour that was richer and more intense than regular cuts of tuna. The meat, particularly near the jaw, was tender and infused with a natural fattiness, giving it a slightly sweet, savoury taste. The texture of meat was a mix of tender and slightly chewy. The collagen near the jawbone had a gelatinous texture. It had a smoky, salty flavour enhanced further with the soy sauce, chilli, and calamansi dip served with it. It was the best lunch Sarah had had, and she didn't scrimp on rice. Benito laughed at her huge appetite.

'I've never been happier,' Sarah rubbed her tummy.

'I'm glad you loved it. This won't be your last gastronomical treat here. I'm having more packed up for our picnic at the waterfall.'

'Sounds absolutely heavenly.'

'How'd your interview go?'

'It went very well.'

'See. I told you you'd ace it!'

They took a short ferry ride on the sedan that the hotel had arranged for them. From the Santa Ana Wharf, it only took them fifteen minutes to get to Samal Island. The drive through Samal Island's lush landscape was a feast for the eyes. Palm trees gave way to fields of flowers and vast orchards. But what made it truly special was the excitement in the air, the palpable sense of anticipation as they headed towards Hagimit Falls.

'Almost there,' Benito said, gripping the wheel as they navigated the last stretch of winding roads.

Sarah gazed out of the window, taking in the verdant mountains around them. 'It's like a painting's come to life,' she marvelled.

Finally, the car came to a stop at a clearing. The sound of water cascading greeted them before they even had a chance to disembark. Sarah couldn't help but quicken her pace as they walked down the well-trodden path, the air cooler and thick with the mist of waterfalls. The way down to the waterfalls was via a steep concrete staircase. They had to hold on to the railings to keep their balance.

'Listen,' Benito said, stopping her with a gentle touch on her arm.

Sarah closed her eyes for a moment, taking in the symphony of nature—the bubbling brooks, chirping birds, and the powerful, almost rhythmic, crashing of water against rock.

'It's enchanting,' she whispered, opening her eyes.

'Just like you,' Benito said softly, locking eyes with her.

Sarah blushed, her heart soaring.

They reached Hagimit Falls, and it was as breathtaking as she had imagined. Unlike typical waterfalls that plunge from great heights, this one was a wall of water, gracefully flowing down rocky formations like drapery. Ferns and moss lined the rocks, giving a sense of age and permanence to the whole scene. It wasn't just one waterfall, Hagimit Falls was a cluster of low waterfalls. Each waterfall was at most five feet high with little pools at each base.

'Wow,' Sarah said, her voice barely above a whisper.

Benito smiled. 'Let's get closer.'

After renting a small hut where they left their bags and the picnic lunch that the hotel had packed for them, they carefully manoeuvred along the rocks and felt mist envelop them as they reached the first waterfall's base.

Sarah closed her eyes for a moment, letting the cool water splash against her face, her arms, her whole being. She felt as if the waterfall was washing away years of fears and hesitations, leaving her lighter and freer. They didn't expect to get any sun at Hagimit Falls as the entire area was protected by a canopy of trees.

Benito reached for Sarah's hand, and their fingers interlocked, both awash in the sheer beauty of the moment and the connection they felt.

'I can't believe places like this exist,' Sarah said, mesmerized.

'And I can't believe it took me so long to experience this with you,' Benito replied, his voice tinged with regret yet filled with happiness.

Benito picked up a pebble from the basin's bank. It was smooth and bluish grey with white speckles. He handed it over to Sarah solemnly.

'What did you learn from this little one?' he asked.

'Some moments are just worth the wait,' Sarah replied, looking deeply into Benito's eyes.

They stood there for what felt like an eternity, lost in the beauty of the world around them and the new-found depth in their relationship.

After their emotional and invigorating time at Hagimit Falls, Benito and Sarah returned to the car, both silently carrying the impact of what they had experienced. Benito turned the key, and the engine roared to life.

'Ready for the next stop?' he asked, a playful edge to his voice.

Sarah smiled. 'Absolutely. What's next?'

'It's another surprise.'

They reached the city centre, a bustling hive of activity. Tricycles zipped by, market stalls lined the streets, and the aroma of grilled meats and fresh fruits wafted through the air. Benito parked the car and led Sarah to a fruit stand filled with an assortment of local produce.

'Ever tried durian?' he asked, picking up the spiky, strong-smelling fruit.

Sarah wrinkled her nose. 'I've heard about it but never tried it. They say you either love it or hate it.'

'Only one way to find out,' Benito said, getting a small chunk and handing her a piece.

She took a tentative bite. The creamy texture and complex flavours surprised her—sweet yet savoury, bold yet delicate. She chewed slowly, savouring it.

'It's incredible,' Sarah said, her eyes widening. 'I never thought it would taste this good.'

Benito laughed, genuinely delighted. 'It's an acquired taste for many, but looks like you're a natural.'

They explored more, walking hand in hand through the streets of Davao. They visited Aldevinco Shopping Centre, famous for its local crafts, and bought a few souvenirs. They also made a quick stop at People's Park, admiring the sculptures and taking a leisurely stroll around the pond.

As evening set in, they found themselves at the seafront, watching the sun dip below the horizon, the sky ablaze with shades of orange and purple.

'You know, I had a feeling that today would be special, but I had no idea it would be this perfect,' Sarah said, leaning her head on Benito's shoulder.

Benito looked at her, his eyes searching hers. 'Life is full of surprises, but sometimes the best moments are those we never saw coming.'

She nodded, her eyes meeting his. 'I couldn't agree more.'

The night descended upon them, yet the city was alive with lights and sounds. But for Sarah and Benito, the world had shrunk to this very moment—encapsulated in the beauty of natural wonders, the taste of new experiences, and the simple yet profound joy of discovering them together.

'One last stop,' Benito said with a smile.

'Another surprise?'

'Davao is full of surprises.'

Benito and Sarah sat on the hood of the car, parked at a viewpoint overlooking Davao City. The evening lights sparkled like jewels in the darkness, illuminating the sprawling urban landscape.

'This is one of my favourite spots,' Benito said. 'It's perfect for introspection. But it's better at the amphitheatre.'

'The amphitheatre?'

'You'll see. We're at Jack's Ridge. It was an outpost of the retreating Japanese forces during World War II. They were forced to beat a path to Matina Hills where they had a commanding view of the outpost where the American ships were anchored. The American soldiers were able to drive them away later, but their fierce battle left many war remnants that can still be found in the area.'

Sarah smiled. 'It's spectacular. And thank you for the little history lesson.'

'I'm in real estate. It pays to know all these little details about a city.'

Benito led Sarah to the amphitheatre. It featured a semi-circular design, common to many amphitheatres, allowing for excellent acoustics and visibility. The seating area was arranged in ascending tiers, providing a clear view of the stage from any point.

'People book this place for weddings,' Benito said.

'Ah, I see!'

Benito took her to the upper edge, leading her to a wooden bench that overlooked the twinkling lights of Davao City.

'Benito, this view. It's priceless! Thank you for all the surprises. It's been wonderful exploring Davao with you.'

'Surprises are a bit like durian, aren't they?' Benito said and grinned.

Sarah laughed. 'What do you mean?'

'Some people can't stand them, and for others, it's an acquired taste. But once you find someone who appreciates them the way you do, it's pretty special.'

Sarah looked at him, her eyes reflecting the city lights. 'I guess we both like something that's not everyone's cup of tea.'

'Yeah,' Benito said, pausing. 'Speaking of which, where do you see your life going, Sarah? With all the water under the bridge, the lost time . . . what's next for you?'

She looked away, pondering. 'I've been asking myself the same question. The work that I thought I loved is gone. Pete broke up with me and I thought we were, you know, going to settle down. Life is up in the air.'

'Do you still consider settling down?'

She met his gaze. 'I used to think about it a lot when I was younger. Not so much recently, but today . . . today reminded me of what could be. What about you?'

'I've had my fair share of relationships, but none of them felt like they were heading towards forever. But who knows, maybe one day I'll find something worth sticking around for.'

'Like durian,' Sarah said, half-jokingly.

'Exactly like durian,' Benito agreed. 'Something or someone that I can't get enough of, no matter what others think.'

Their eyes met, and for a moment, the world around them ceased to exist. Benito broke the silence.

'You know, I used to visit these places with my family when I was a kid. And I always imagined coming back one day, sharing them with someone who'd appreciate them as much as I do.'

Sarah felt her heart swell. 'And did you find that person?'

'I think I might have,' he said softly.

Just then, a fireworks display erupted over the city, casting a magical glow over the landscape. Both of them took it as a sign, an affirmation of the unspoken connection that had blossomed between them. There was no holiday. But someone out there in Davao City was celebrating something, just like Sarah and Benito.

As the last firework faded away, Benito turned to Sarah. 'So, where do we go from here?'

She smiled, her eyes sparkling, 'Let's keep exploring, Benito. Together.'

'Sounds like a plan,' he said.

They got back into the car and headed to their hotel.

'Today might have been an unexpected delay, but it's made me more certain about what I want in my future.'

'And what's that?' Sarah asked, her voice tinged with hope.

'A life full of adventure, love, and yes—lots of durian.' Benito grinned.

Sarah chuckled. 'Well, you're in luck. I happen to love all those things.' After a brief pause, she said, 'I want to ask you something, Benito.'

'What is it?'

'I'm not sure about this job interview.'

'What do you mean? Wasn't that what you wanted?'

'Yes, it was. But, I'm not so sure now. This trip was really eye-opening. My blog has been getting a lot of followers.'

'That's awesome. But what does it have to do with your job interview?'

'I was thinking of doing something else.'

'Like what?'

'Like starting my own business.'

'Whoa. That's a huge decision. Is it something you're really ready for?'

'Hey, that's easy for you to say. You've never had to apply for a job.'

'That's unfair, Sarah.'

Sarah could feel it again, Benito's hot-headed side. She didn't want to get into a fight. Not after such a lovely day with him.

'Look, let's not talk about it any more. Forget that I brought it up.'

'No, Sarah. I want to talk about it.'

'Not while you're upset.'

'I don't understand! What's so wrong with being upset? Am I not allowed to get upset?' Benito didn't raise his voice, but he was clearly riled.

'That's not what I said!'

'Then, be honest. What did you mean about me never having to apply for a job?' Benito darted a look at her but quickly looked back at the road ahead.

Sarah sighed. 'I'm sorry. I didn't mean it that way. But it's true, right? You didn't have to apply for your job.'

'That's not how our family business works, Sarah. You've never had to see it first-hand, but all of us have had to prove to our dad that we're capable. We all had to start at the bottom.'

'I'm sorry. I didn't know that.'

'That's why I asked you if you were ready to own a business. It's really tough. The risks are personal. You're responsible for more than yourself.'

'I got it, Benito.'

'You know, Sarah, fighting isn't always bad. Healthy couples *should* fight.'

'Should they?'

'There's a study on it,' Benito said seriously. Sarah nodded. Benito broke into his characteristic grin.

'I don't know if there's a study on it. My parents fight a lot. They try to keep it from us kids, but we know. And it's fine. Their marriage is fine. We know they love each other. The fights are temporary. The love is permanent.'

'I like that.'

As they drove back into the heart of Davao City, Sarah knew that while their trip might have been delayed, their journey—filled with the promise of many more shared adventures and delightful discoveries (even disagreements)— was just beginning.

Back in their hotel room, Sarah felt an overwhelming mix of emotions. Benito's candour about his past relationships, his work, and his parents' marriage left her teetering between vulnerability and hope.

'Do you see a future for us, Benito?' she asked, her eyes searching his for reassurance.

Benito took a moment, sensing the importance of his next words. He looked deep into her eyes, brushing a stray hair from her face.

'I've waited a long time for this moment, Sarah. Years of wondering if we'd ever be more than friends, years of not knowing what would come next. In that time, I've had relationships, yes, but none that ever made me forget you. None that made me want to stop waiting for what we could have,' he spoke, his voice unwavering.

'Why'd you wait so long, Benito?' Sarah asked.

'Because I've always known it would be worth it. No one knows you like I do, Sarah. I've seen you through the time your dad left to the time Pete broke up with you. I've seen your one hundred different laughs. I've seen your composed and quiet crying. I've seen your ugly crying. I want to be there for you. All the time.'

He paused, taking her hand in his.

'I can be serious, Sarah. I've never been more serious about anything in my life. If you're willing to take a chance on us, then I promise, you won't regret it.'

Sarah looked at him, her eyes filling with tears of relief and joy. Here was Benito, a man she had known for so many years, yet was getting to know all over again in a deeper way.

'Then show me,' she whispered.

Benito leaned in and kissed her, softly at first, then deepening it as if to seal a sacred pact. It was a kiss that spoke of years of longing, of waiting, of hopes and dreams that could now finally begin to unfold. They held each other close, as if afraid that letting go would make the moment disappear.

Journal entry
Bonus: Hagimit Falls

This waterfall was not part of my itinerary. I had just
planned on visiting seven waterfalls. However, this
particular one is very special to me. It reminds me
that something will always throw off my well-laid
plans. It's okay to have plans. I was a born planner.
However, it's also okay to embrace the unplanned
curveballs life throws at you. There's a gift hidden in
each one. That was exactly what I felt here. Hagimit
Falls in Island Garden City of Samal, Davao del
Norte, may be small, but its beauty is unparalleled. It
is made of a cluster of waterfalls no higher than five
feet high and the water flows from cluster to cluster.
This was one of the most peaceful waterfalls among
them all, a hidden paradise that captivated my heart.

Smooth, bluish-grey stone with white speckles.

Some moments are just worth the wait.

Act 3

The Way Back Home

CHAPTER 27

The sunrise found Sarah and Benito tangled in a sleepy embrace, blissfully unaware that their alarm had failed to rouse them. It wasn't until Sarah's phone buzzed with a text—a reminder of their impending flight—that they snapped awake.

'Oh my God, we overslept!' Sarah's eyes widened in panic.

Benito scrambled to his feet. Benito's eyes darted to the digital clock on the nightstand. 'Sarah, it's 9:15! Our flight!'

Sarah's eyes widened in disbelief. 'No, no, no . . . this can't be happening! We have exactly one hour before the flight leaves. We can make it if we rush.'

Both of them moved at breakneck speed, shoving clothes into bags and quickly running through a mental checklist of essentials. Sarah's meticulous organization—which had earned her the nickname 'Steady Sarah' among friends—was abandoned in the chaos. Benito was already on the phone with the hotel's front desk, his voice urgent. 'We need a ride to the airport, now.'

Minutes ticked away as they waited at the front desk for the car. Benito kept checking with the front desk, contemplating if he should get another ride through an app.

At last, their airport ride arrived, and as they hurriedly checked out of the hotel, neither noticed that Sarah's small bag, filled with her collection of pebbles, had been left behind.

Both Sarah and Benito were on the edge of their seats throughout the ride. Each red light seemed to last an eternity, each stretch of clear road too brief. They checked their phones compulsively, watching the minutes tick away with agonizing slowness.

'We're going to miss it, aren't we?' Sarah muttered, her knuckles white as she clutched her phone.

Benito shook his head. 'No, we're not. We're going to make it. We have to.'

The car sped through the morning mist, but as they neared the airport, Sarah's heart sank. 'We just have ten minutes before the check-in closes.'

'We'll make it,' Benito said, though uncertainty crept into his voice.

The car screeched to a halt outside the terminal, and both Sarah and Benito practically leapt from the backseat. They thanked the driver more hastily than they would have liked. Sarah and Benito sprinted to the check-in counter just as the airline staff was about to close up.

'Made it,' Benito gasped, leaning on the counter.

Sarah's heart was pounding so loudly, she could barely hear the airport announcements.

'Flight to Manila?' the airline representative asked, frowning.

'Yes, yes, that's us!' Sarah exclaimed.

'You've got a couple of minutes. I can check you in, but you need to hurry to the gate,' the representative said, typing hurriedly.

Just as they thought they could finally breathe a sigh of relief, Sarah's face paled. 'Wait. Wait! Where's my other little bag?'

'What?' Benito looked confused, scanning their belongings.

'My small reusable bag! The one with the pebbles from all the waterfalls we visited. It's not here!'

Sarah felt a lump form in her throat. Those pebbles weren't just stones to her; they were mementos, each one marking a special moment of their journey. She felt her eyes prickle with tears. Now, they were gone forever.

Seated in the aircraft, their hands clasped as the plane taxied down the runway. Sarah and Benito felt a sense of exhaustion and relief wash over them. They had made it, against all odds. But as the plane soared into the air, Sarah's thoughts returned to the missing bag and the pebbles it contained.

Benito noticed her disquiet. 'What's wrong?'

'This isn't like me,' Sarah confessed, her voice tinged with disbelief. 'I'm "Steady Sarah", remember?'

Benito chuckled. 'Well, maybe "Steady Sarah" needed a little shake-up.'

Sarah sighed. 'It's not just a bag, you know? Each of those pebbles was a piece of this adventure, a piece of us.'

Benito nodded, taking a moment before speaking. 'But maybe that's just it. We collect these things, these mementos, because they hold meaning. But in the end, the real meaning is in the experience, in the shared moments. Those can't be lost because they're a part of us now.'

Sarah looked at Benito, her eyes meeting his. For the first time since the morning's chaos, she felt truly calm. 'You're right. We'll always have Davao, and all the other places we visited, locked safely in our memories. And our adventure doesn't end here.'

Benito squeezed her hand, smiling. 'Exactly. Missing a bag is a little loss, but what we've gained is so much greater. We've got a lifetime of waterfalls, trails, and yes, even almost-missed flights and lost luggage to look forward to.'

As the plane soared above the clouds, Sarah found herself smiling. She had spent so many years clinging to stability and routine; maybe it was time to let go.

'Benito, do you ever think about how our lives are like luggage?' she mused, looking out at the endless sky. 'We carry around so much "stuff" that we think is important, but when we lose some, we realize how little we actually need to be happy.'

He intertwined his fingers with hers. 'Then consider this lost bag a lesson. You've got everything you truly need right here,' he gestured between them, 'and in here,' he touched her heart.

Sarah felt a warmth spread through her, pushing away any lingering regret about her lost pebbles. She turned to Benito, her eyes brighter than they'd ever been.

'So, what's our next big adventure?' she asked, her voice tinged with excitement.

'You're Sarah, the Seeker. I think it won't be long until you come up with the next one.'

They both laughed, a shared laughter that filled the tiny space between their airplane seats and seemed to radiate throughout the cabin. As they leaned in for a kiss, Sarah felt a sense of profound gratitude. For the places they had visited, for the little losses that taught them big lessons, but most of all, for the person beside her, with whom she could face any loss and still feel like the richest person in the world.

'And just think,' Benito whispered as they pulled apart, 'this is only the beginning.'

Sarah smiled, her eyes shining bright, 'You're absolutely right.'

Sarah knew that the 'stuff' she'd left behind paled in comparison to the love and the sense of adventure that she'd gained. The world below them had never seemed so full of endless possibilities.

But going home also meant having to face difficult situations. She had a job interview pending. Did she really want that job now? What was she going to do about her mom's secret? How long would Miguel be in the dark? Before she left for South Cotabato, her mom had said something cryptic about needing to talk. What did she want to talk about? What if she wanted her to meet her dad? Was she ready?

I don't know.

She would be going back to reality soon. As the plane descended towards Manila, Sarah looked out of the window, not just at the sprawling city beneath them, but at the endless horizon stretching beyond it. She had a lot to think about when they landed, but at least she had this now: a horizon full of adventures yet to come, and a life's worth of little losses and immeasurable gains.

CHAPTER 28

Sarah couldn't believe it took less than two hours to fly from Davao to Manila. It was just a fraction of what she spent travelling by sea and by land to get to Cebu, Bohol, Siquijor, Camiguin, Cagayan de Oro, and South Cotabato.

'Hey, sleepyhead, we're home,' Sarah poked Benito in the ribs. This was another thing Sarah did not foresee at all, this wonderful, crazy, precious thing she had with Benito. He'd been her friend since forever but being his girlfriend (there was that word again, Sarah wished there was another word for it) was scary and exciting and wonderful, all at the same time. He hadn't shaved since Bohol and his cheeks and chin were all stubbly but Sarah couldn't help kissing him anyway.

'Whoa! That woke me up,' Benito said, touching her cheek. 'Are you ready to go home to reality?' he asked her.

'Ugh. Not yet. I have a million and one things that I still need to do. Don't remind me just yet.'

'Like what?'

'Like getting a new job?'

'You know, I think I need a personal assistant at my office . . .' Benito said, running his hand lightly over her left arm.

There he went again, turning her on. It didn't take much from him. All he needed to do was touch her.

'Benito, stop teasing! I'm serious. And no, I'm not working for you. Tack that onto your brain. Let's just talk about something else.'

'Eddie will pick us up at the airport.' Eddie was Benito's family driver. 'Let's drop you off first, okay?'

'Okay.'

'So, do you think your mom will still let me hang out in your bedroom now that we're together?'

'Benito!' Sarah hit him with a rolled-up in-flight magazine.

'Come in, Benito,' Helen said when he dropped Sarah off at her place. Benito stepped down from the car and kissed her mom.

'Tita Helen, I won't any more, if you don't mind. I have to go home and freshen up. I'll be back later in the afternoon.'

'Oh, I need to talk to Sarah. Come by for dinner instead.'

'Okay, Tita!'

What did they need to talk about?

'I missed you, Ate!' Miguel said as he met her at the door.

'I missed you too, bro.'

Miguel hugged Sarah tightly.

'How's your ankle, Ate?'

'It's perfectly fine. There's just an ugly mark but that's all.'

'Sarah, go unpack. I'll get lunch going in a bit. The rice will be ready in a few minutes. We need to talk.'

'Okay, Ma!'

There was that mention of 'talk' again. Sarah was getting concerned. She didn't have much to unpack so she proceeded to the kitchen to help out her mom.

'What are we talking about, Ma?'

'Your dad is coming here after lunch.'

'What?' What a homecoming! 'Why didn't you tell me earlier?'

'I'm telling you now.'

'Why, Ma? What for?'

'He's been wanting to talk to you for the longest time. Now is as good a time as any.'

'But, Ma, I just got back. I want to spend time with you and Miguel.'

'This has been long overdue, Sarah.'

'What about Miguel?'

'Sarah, your dad has been visiting Miguel. It's just you that he hasn't talked to.'

Sarah was shocked.

'How long has he been seeing Miguel?'

'Just at the start of summer break. They go biking too, you know.'

'Miguel never mentioned this.' Sarah's head was starting to ache. She set down the plates on the dining table and paused.

'He didn't want to upset you.'

Well, she *was* upset. She felt betrayed.

Her mom set her chicken adobo on the table, but Sarah saw tears in her eyes.

'I'm glad I cooked this earlier because I would have spoiled it—' Helen said, her voice cracking. Sarah hugged her mom.

'Stop it, Ma. It's okay.' She thought of her speech to Benito, that night in Camiguin, about love. Sarah realized she wasn't treating her mom the way she should be. What was *this* in the face of all the sacrifices her mom made for her?

'I love you, Mama. If this is something you want. I'll do it.' *I'll do it even if it hurts.*

'I didn't want to have to call your dad to tell him not to come.' Her mom was crying in earnest.

'Tell him to come. It's okay.'

When the doorbell rang at 2.30, Sarah knew it was her dad. She had panicked over what to wear but she realized she was just being ridiculous. She could wear whatever she damn well pleased. She heard her mom open the door for her dad.

Sarah entered the sala and saw her dad stand up as soon as he saw her.

'Sarah, Jorge, I'll leave you two to talk, okay?' Helen said.

'Thank you, Helen,' her dad said. She remembered that voice. She hadn't heard it since she was seven. Sarah felt surreal seeing her dad again after such a long time. But she didn't feel the righteous anger she was expecting to feel. It was something different, something akin to weariness and a little bit of relief. The latter came as a surprise to her.

Her dad had always been handsome. He was still that way. He stood up straight, his hair, now salt and pepper, was still thick and neatly combed back. He was wearing a light-pink collared shirt and dark-coloured pants.

'How are you, Sarah?' he asked. He sounded apprehensive, stiff. Sarah felt the same way, actually.

'Do you want anything . . . Dad?' She wasn't sure how it would come out of her mouth. But that was what she called him before. It felt weird to be saying it again.

'Oh. Just water.'

Sarah went back to the kitchen and fetched a pitcher of water from the refrigerator and a couple of glasses. She brought them back in a tray and set it down on the table between them. *Help yourself.* But she didn't say it aloud.

'I just came back from a trip down south,' Sarah said. Small talk. She couldn't believe it.

'Your mom told me about it. How was it?'

'Enlightening.' One word. It was true, though. 'Sorry, Dad, but I want to cut to the chase. What are you doing here? After all this time?'

Her dad's face looked stricken.

'Sarah, I came here to ask for your forgiveness,' her dad said. His hands were stretched out, as if he wanted to bridge the distance between them.

'I've waited a very long time to hear that,' Sarah said, 'But don't expect me to keel over because of this one visit.' For the first time, she realized, she was talking to him, adult to adult.

'I'm not expecting anything, Sarah. I just wanted to see you . . . to see how you're doing. I want you to know that I'm here for you. I didn't want to wait until it was too late.'

'Too late for what?'

'Too late to be in your life any more.' *Was it too late?*

'Why now, Dad? What's changed?'

'Sarah, I've always wanted to see you and Miguel, but I made a mistake. I'm not sure I can completely explain right now. I knew you and Miguel needed your mom more. I thought I would just get in the way.' *What kind of thinking was that?*

'Dad, it was your *choice*!'

'I know that, Sarah. I'm sorry. I'm so sorry.'

She could see tears glistening in her dad's eyes.

'You have a whole different life that Miguel and I are not part of.' Sarah was just stating the obvious. But it still hurt.

'I *want* you to be a part of it.'

'Dad, you can't just show up here seventeen years later and—' It was Sarah's turn to cry. It *was* seventeen years, the same age as Miguel. It was a lifetime. What was he expecting, anyway?

'Sarah, even though your mom and I had our differences, we've come to be friends—'

'We didn't deserve what you did to us!'

'None of you did. I tried my best—'

'It's just money, Dad.' Yes, she *was* grateful. She'd always been. But that gratitude always came with a bitter price, a father-shaped hole that had gotten deeper and deeper over the years. Sarah realized, all of a sudden, that this was where all her money issues had stemmed from.

'I know it was a poor way to show you that I still cared, that I still care.'

'Do you, Dad?'

'I always will. I swore to your mother that I would take care of you and Miguel. I'm sorry if I couldn't be there for you. God knows how much I wanted to be there for you, physically. But I'll always take care of you, Miguel, and your mother, no matter what.' Tears were falling down his cheeks and he didn't bother to wipe them away any more. 'I don't know if you'll ever understand how sorry I am, Sarah.'

Through the haze of pain that resurfaced in Sarah's heart on seeing her father again, she knew that her dad was sincere.

He didn't have to do anything. He had the upper hand, after all, holding up the bargain for child support and more. She felt a thorn leave her heart, but it was still bleeding.

'Dad,' she said slowly, 'I don't really know you that well.' It was a fact.

'Can we start there, Sarah? Can I come see you and Miguel?'

'We can start there.'

'Sarah, you don't even have to call me dad. I don't deserve the title. But please believe me when I say I want to earn it.'

It was Sarah who breached the distance between them and embraced him. Knowing what she knew, she realized she had to give her dad a chance.

'Thank you for telling me it's not too late, anak,' Jorge said.

'And thank you for taking care of us, in your own way, Dad. But I'm serious about the time that you owe us.'

'You have it, Sarah.'

CHAPTER 29

Sarah's phone buzzed on the coffee table, breaking the stillness of the early afternoon. She reached over and unlocked the screen to see a text from Pete: *Hey Sarah, I've transferred your share from our joint account to your savings. However, for the insurance bit, I'll need to get back to you. There will be some paperwork. Best of luck, Pete.*

The message was curt, devoid of the warmth they once shared. As she stared at the words on the screen, a whirlpool of emotions surged within her, memories of a shared past clouding her vision. She sighed, putting her phone down. It was funny how a simple message could make her feel like a chapter of her life had closed for good.

She thought about the condo they had wanted to invest in—a symbol of their shared dreams and aspirations, the love they once felt for each other encapsulated in concrete, glass, and meticulous interior design. It was supposed to be their haven, their piece of paradise in the frenetic bustle of Manila. But now, it was just another place, disconnected from her current life.

A dream had ended. Or maybe, it had merely transformed, reshaping itself to fit her new reality.

Sarah sat there for a moment, contemplating the complexity of feelings that came with endings and new beginnings. She was not the same person who had excitedly discussed colour palettes and furniture choices with Pete. And that was okay.

She picked up her phone again and replied: *Thank you, Pete. I wish you all the best too.*

Sarah felt a mixture of relief and resignation. It was the final tie that needed severing, the last remnant of a shared future that would never come to be. With the joint account settled, Pete was well and truly part of her past. With that, she let go of a dream that was no longer hers.

On impulse, she hailed a cab and directed it to the development where their future home was supposed to be.

Sarah found herself standing in front of the sleek, glassy façade of the condo building. Taking a deep breath, she walked through the lobby and made her way to the showroom, her heels clicking softly on the marble floor.

The showroom hadn't changed. It still exuded the same aura of promise and potential. She could almost hear her past self bubbling with excitement, envisioning a life of settled bliss with Pete.

As she stepped inside, a wave of nostalgia washed over her. The same stylish furniture, the same optimistic layout promising comfort and luxury, greeted her eyes. She could almost hear echoes of her past excitement, conversations filled with plans for a future that was never to be.

She remembered the day she and Pete had visited this showroom for the first time. Their eyes had sparkled with the same enthusiasm, their hands interlocking as if to confirm the silent pact that they were building a life together. Back then, the condo represented a milestone, a shared accomplishment. But now, it was a monument to a dream deferred, an avenue that split into two separate paths.

Sarah walked through the living room, her fingertips grazing the plush fabric of the couch, the cool surface of the granite kitchen counter. Each touch felt like a goodbye, a release of something that had once held so much importance but was no longer relevant.

She stopped in front of a large window, gazing out at the Manila skyline. How many nights had she envisioned watching the sunset here with Pete, embracing the comforts and challenges of adulthood together? But dreams, she realized, were not set in stone; they were mutable, evolving with the people who dreamed them.

Taking one last look around, Sarah smiled softly. She wasn't sad, nor did she feel regret. Rather, she felt grateful for the memories, even if they were no longer her reality. She was saying goodbye to one dream to make room for another, a new vision that included adventures with Benito, and a different kind of love, passionate yet grounded in shared goals and ideals.

'Thank you,' she whispered to the empty room, her voice tinged with reverence for the past and anticipation for the future. With that, she turned and walked out of the showroom, her heels clicking in a steady rhythm that sounded a lot like freedom.

'Good afternoon, ma'am. Are you interested in one of our units?' A sales agent broke her reverie.

Sarah shook her head. 'No, just reminiscing.'

She stood there for a few more moments, her eyes sweeping over the elegantly designed space. It was still a beautiful condo, but it no longer represented her dreams. Finally, she took a deep breath.

'Goodbye,' she whispered, not to the condo, but to the vision of life she'd once coveted. She stepped out of the showroom, feeling lighter.

Her phone rang.

'Hi, Sarah! It's me, Jilian.'

'Oh, hi, Jilian!'

'Are you back in Manila?'

'Yes, I am.'

'Are you free on Friday for an in-person interview?'

Sarah hesitated.

'Yes, I'm free.'

'Great. Would you be able to come to our office at 4.00 p.m.?'

'Yes, that's fine with me.'

'I'll take care of printing out your CV. No need to bring it on Friday. I'll also email you a link to an online behavioural competency analysis. Just standard procedure.'

'Thanks, Jilian.'

'See you on Friday, 4.00 p.m.'

She thought she had said goodbye to her old life. But here it was, giving her a call.

What do I really want?

Sarah arrived home, her thoughts still lingering on the emotional farewell she had given to her old dream. As she stepped inside, the aroma of a home-cooked meal wafted through the air, grounding her in the present.

'Ma, I'm home,' she called out, hanging her purse on the hook by the door.

Helen emerged from the kitchen, wiping her hands on a dishtowel. 'There you are.' She immediately noticed Sarah's contemplative mood.

'You look like you're miles away,' Helen remarked, 'Want to talk about it?'

Sarah sighed. 'I was just thinking about how our dreams change over time. You know, you wanted a different life when Dad was still around, didn't you?'

Helen paused, choosing her words carefully. 'Yes, dreams change, often because we change. Your father and I had dreams that didn't include the realities we later had to face. When he left, I had to focus on what was immediate and necessary—you and your brother.'

Sarah hesitated before diving in. 'Ma, did you ever have dreams that you had to give up for something—or someone—else?'

Helen took a seat across from her, a serious look on her face. 'Oh, plenty. Life is full of turns and choices. Sometimes, the dreams you had have to be adjusted, or even let go, for something more immediate or important.'

'Ma, I have a job interview on Friday.'

'Anak, that's great!' Helen reached out for Sarah's hand.

'But, Ma, I don't know if I still want the same job I had before.'

'I thought that was what you wanted. Weren't you sending out your résumé for that job?'

'I was. But after my trip, I was thinking of doing something different.'

'What were you thinking of?'

'Starting my own business. I already called Marley about it, and she was excited to do it with me.'

Helen looked at Sarah and held her hand.

'I want you to choose what's best for you.'

'Aren't you going to tell me to go for what's practical?'

'Yes, that would make sense. But this is your life, anak. I'll be here to support you, whatever you choose.'

'Thank you, Ma,' Sarah squeezed her mom's hand.

Sarah's mind drifted to her father. 'Why didn't you ever look for Miguel's dad after he left?'

Her mom sighed, her eyes growing distant. 'It's complicated. At the time, I thought I loved him. But when I found myself alone, taking care of two children, I realized that some dreams—some loves—are not meant to be pursued. My priority became you and Miguel, and the family we already had.'

'But don't you think Miguel has the right to know about his biological dad?'

Helen's eyes met Sarah's. 'Yes, he does. And when the time is right, I'll have that conversation with him. But it has to be on my terms, in my own time. It's a conversation that needs a lot of preparation.'

Sarah felt a pang of frustration, yet she understood her mother's perspective. 'He's almost an adult, Mom. The right time is coming sooner than you think.'

'I know,' Helen said softly. 'But there are things you'll understand when you're a parent. For now, trust me.'

Sarah sighed. 'I trust you, Ma. But Miguel deserves to know the truth. Whenever you're ready, I'll support your decision. Just don't keep it from him forever, okay? Miguel has a right to know.'

She gave her mom a hug.

After the conversation with her mom, Sarah retreated to her room, feeling a deeper understanding of how life's complexities could alter her most cherished plans. Her phone buzzed, snapping her out of her thoughts.

Benito: *On my way. Ready for our date?*

A smile spread across Sarah's face, widening as she typed her reply. *Absolutely. Can't wait.*

As she put down her phone, she realized that her conversation with her mom had further solidified her new-found outlook. Life was a patchwork of different dreams, some realized, others forsaken, yet all meaningful. And she was ready to weave a new pattern into hers, coloured with the shades of her future adventures with Benito.

Sarah felt a surge of hope and excitement, the kind that she hadn't felt in a long time. The condo with Pete represented a dream lost, but what she had found in Benito was an entirely different but equally beautiful dream.

When Benito arrived to pick her up, Sarah was ready to step into a new chapter of her life, one she hadn't planned for but was now eager to write. Their eyes met and they both knew, without a word spoken, that they were embarking on a new dream together.

Sarah closed the door behind her, leaving her old dreams to rest as she moved forward, her heart full and her eyes set on the uncharted path ahead. She knew it would have its share of challenges, but for the first time in her life, the unpredictability of it all did not seem daunting, but thrilling. It was a different dream, a spontaneous dream, but it was hers—and now, also Benito's. And that made all the difference in the world.

CHAPTER 30

Sarah was dressed in her best corporate attire, tailored black blazer, beige silk blouse, black trousers, and black block heels. Despite Jilian having told her that she would print her résumé, Sarah still brought a black portfolio with several copies of her CV inside. Nothing wrong with over-preparing. She'd decided to still show up to her interview. It was her philosophy to not close doors. 'Consider it practice for doing a pitch,' she had told herself.

The lobby of Ascentra Connect was elegant, if a bit cold, with black marble and chrome accents. Jilian greeted her with a warm smile.

'Nice to see you in person, Sarah. You look great,' Jilian said.

'Thanks, Jilian. I love your blouse,' Sarah smiled. She *did* love Jilian's blouse. It was an immaculate white seersucker tunic that looked both professional and feminine.

'Thanks, Sarah! Please follow me. You'll be interviewed by our director of accounts, Kevin Rodriguez.' Sarah suddenly got the jitters again. She took deep breaths.

Kevin's office was grey-themed, neat, and orderly. He had a shelf full of business books behind his desk. But what caught Sarah's eye was a framed photo of his family in Santorini, Greece.

I want to go there.

Jilian introduced Sarah to Kevin and then took her leave.

'Have a seat, Sarah,' Kevin said with a smile. He had a close-cropped haircut and looked fit. 'Jilian had a lot of great things to say about you. I won't really ask you to run through your résumé again. I know you're more than capable. I'd like to know more about you, the Sarah who's not on these pages,' he indicated the paper on his desk.

Sarah smiled. She was ready.

'I just came back from a trip to find seven waterfalls, each one hidden and tough to reach, but each one worth the trek. It was a real adventure, not unlike my own career path. I'm sure Jilian has mentioned this to you. I was retrenched from my previous job. It was a shock to me, like suddenly hitting a dead end on a familiar trail. But instead of turning back, I saw it as a detour, a chance to explore new paths. Each waterfall I reached reminded me that I'm built to face challenges head-on, to adapt and keep moving forward.

'In my last job, I was known for delivering results, even when the pressure was on. I believe it's not just about what you do but how you handle the unexpected twists. Now, I'm here, ready to bring that same resilience and problem-solving attitude to your team. This opportunity feels like the next step in a journey I'm excited to take, a new challenge I'm ready to tackle head-first. I think that's the kind of spirit and dedication Ascentra Connect values, and I'm eager to show what I can bring to the table.'

Kevin leaned forward. 'That's quite an attitude, Sarah. I'm really impressed. Yes, Jilian did mention this to me, but hearing it from you is even better.'

'It's been quite the ride,' Sarah said.

'I won't beat around the bush much. It's clear to me that you're a fit at Ascentra. Your position is going to have more challenges because you're not just going to be a team leader. You'll be handling more than one account. Is this something you're up to?'

'I love challenges.'

'Well, that's great then.'

'I have to be honest with you, though, Kevin. I'm also still evaluating more options.'

'Is it another BPO? I think you know that Ascentra is one of the best, if not *the* best in the industry. Our benefits are unrivalled.'

'I want to put up my own business.'

'Well, that's really gutsy, Sarah.'

'That's what I've been told.'

'Give Ascentra a lot of thought. This is a great company. It shouldn't stop you from thinking about your business. That might be something you might want to do in a couple of years down the road. We like entrepreneurial-minded people here.'

'Thanks, Kevin. I'll give this a lot of thought.'

Sarah left the interview feeling empowered. When she had nothing to lose, it made her feel more free to make a choice. What Kevin said made a lot of sense. What was she going to do? *This is a good problem*, she reminded herself.

CHAPTER 31

Sarah checked her face on her compact mirror as her ride pulled up in front of the quaint café, a quiet place nestled between high-rise buildings and crowded streets. Today, she felt a soft anticipation vibrating through her bones. She was meeting her father, Jorge, in a setting that neither of them had ever anticipated—two grown adults navigating the complicated maze of a fractured relationship. It had been two months since she last saw him. She thought it was about time to meet him again.

Jorge was already waiting at a corner table, sipping on what looked like black coffee. He glanced up and smiled as Sarah entered the café. As she approached him, he stood up, ever the gentleman.

'Hey, Dad,' Sarah greeted, a tinge of nervousness lacing her voice. She didn't know if she should kiss him on the cheek or something. She decided against it. He pulled out a chair for her.

Jorge sat opposite her, his eyes showing signs of age but still radiating warmth. 'You look beautiful, Sarah,' he began.

'You don't look too bad yourself, Dad,' she replied, steadying her shaking voice.

They sat down, and a waitress approached to take their orders. Sarah went for an herbal tea while Jorge stuck with his coffee. The quiet between them was less tense now, but Sarah knew they had some boulders to remove from their path.

A moment of silence filled the space between them. 'I've missed moments like these, anak,' Jorge finally said.

Sarah met his gaze, seeing a vulnerability she hadn't noticed before. 'I've missed them too, Dad. More than you'll ever know,' she confessed. A pause lingered, heavy yet liberating.

'I talked to Ma, Dad. She told me everything,' Sarah finally broke the silence, her words heavy in the air.

Jorge looked at his hands, intertwined on his lap. 'I see. And how does that make you feel?'

'I understand why you had to go,' Sarah said, her voice tinged with acceptance. 'Ma was lonely, and you were always busy. Miguel happened, and you couldn't stay. But you kept supporting us, anyway.'

Jorge's voice was a mix of regret and relief as he admitted, 'I couldn't bear the thought of not being a part of your lives, even Miguel's. However, at that time, I decided that you needed your mom more than me. I just couldn't be in the same house with your mom.'

'That's why I'm so confused, Dad,' Sarah said softly. 'You supported us. You've treated Miguel as your own. But, you weren't around, physically.'

'Miguel may not be my biological son, but he's still a part of this family. Just like I've always considered you my daughter, even when I wasn't physically there.'

'That's what I don't understand. Why couldn't you stay . . . for our sake? Mine and Miguel's?'

Jorge was silent.

'I'm sorry, Sarah. There's really no way around it. I made a mistake when I decided that I couldn't be in the same house as your mom.'

Sarah sighed. She understood why, but . . .

'It's like you didn't love us enough to stay.' Sarah knew her words would hurt him. But she needed him to hear those words.

Jorge bowed his head. 'I can't take that back. I can't take back all that time. I thought I was the one making the sacrifice. But you're right. I was the selfish one.'

Sarah was surprised to hear him admit that he had been selfish.

'Dad, I've spent years being angry, blaming you for everything that happened. I used to think, how could you leave us? But after hearing Mom's side of the story, I understand. I do. You chose to do the wrong thing, but that's water under the bridge now. As you said, we can't do it over any more. But, I think it's time to mend what's broken.'

Jorge's eyes filled with tears he no longer wanted to hold back. 'I've been waiting for years to hear you say that, Sarah. I know I can't turn back time, but I hope we can rebuild from here. Thank you, Sarah. That means the world to me.'

Sarah continued, 'I think it's time for you and Mom to start seeing other people. You both deserve happiness, even if it's not with each other.'

Jorge chuckled. 'I never thought I'd hear my daughter giving me dating advice.'

'Well, times have changed,' Sarah grinned.

Jorge nodded, contemplating his daughter's words. 'Maybe you're right. Your mom and I are both at a place where we can finally accept what happened. Maybe it's time to move on.'

For a moment, they sat in silence, absorbed in their own thoughts but comforted by the warmth of their healing relationship.

Jorge looked at Sarah, sensing there was more on her mind. 'You look like you have something else you want to talk about,' he ventured.

Sarah hesitated for a moment, looking across her, families enjoying their day, couples sharing tables for two. She then took a deep breath and turned back to her father. 'I don't want to make the same mistakes you did, Dad,' she began cautiously.

Jorge's eyes narrowed a little, but he knew this was a conversation that needed to happen. 'Go on,' he encouraged.

'You gave your all to your career, and it cost you your family. I have so many opportunities ahead of me, but I don't want to look back one day and realize that I've lost the people I love,' Sarah expressed, her words heavy with the burden of the future.

Jorge sighed, contemplating his daughter's words. 'You're right, Sarah. I let my ambitions blind me to what was really important. And by the time I realized it, it was too late. Your mother had already found comfort in the arms of another man, and I couldn't completely blame her.'

'So, how do I avoid that? How do I balance a fulfilling career with a meaningful personal life?' Sarah asked, almost pleading for some kind of blueprint to avoid the pitfalls that entrapped her parents.

Jorge looked deep into her eyes, wishing he had all the answers. 'There's no foolproof plan, anak. But one thing I can tell you is to never take the people you love for granted. Always make time for them, no matter how busy you get.'

'But what if making time means sacrificing opportunities?' Sarah pressed.

Jorge thought about it carefully before responding, 'Then you have to ask yourself what truly matters most to you. Sometimes, missing an opportunity could be the best thing that happens to you if it means preserving something far more precious. Oh, Sarah, if there's one thing I wish I could redo, it's balancing my time between work and family. I thought providing financially was the most important thing. I was wrong. So, my advice to you is simple: don't make your work your entire world. Make time for the people who matter. I'm the least qualified to give you this advice because I have so many regrets.'

Sarah nodded, absorbing her father's advice. 'It's okay, Dad. We're here now, talking. It took a while, but we eventually got here. I want to be there for Benito, for Miguel, for Ma, and for you. I want to cherish the people who make life worth living.'

Jorge's face softened, his eyes brimming with pride and a little sorrow. 'I wish I had understood that sooner, Sarah. But I'm glad you're realizing it now. I've learned that success is not just what you accomplish in your life; it's also about what you inspire others to do.'

Sarah felt a tear slide down her cheek as she embraced her father. 'Thank you, Dad. I do. I do want to make time for the people who matter to me most.'

Jorge hugged her back tightly, his eyes moist but his heart lighter than it had felt in years. 'That's all a parent could ever wish for,' he whispered.

As they pulled away from the embrace, Sarah felt a new-found sense of clarity. 'Dad, let's promise to spend more time together. Maybe I could join you and Miguel for one of your weekend outings?'

Jorge's eyes lit up at the suggestion. 'I'd love that, Sarah. Miguel would be thrilled too.'

'Speaking of Miguel,' Sarah hesitated, searching for the right words, 'do you think it's time he knew the truth about his biological father?'

Jorge's face grew solemn, his eyes gazing into the distance as if looking for an answer. 'That's a very sensitive matter, Sarah. I think your mom will know what to do when the time is right. On this one, I'd leave it entirely up to her.'

Sarah nodded, understanding the gravity of her father's words. 'You're right, Dad. But I do hope that, whatever happens, we can still be a family. A real family.'

Jorge looked at his daughter, his eyes reflecting the complexity of the years gone by and the uncertainty of what lay ahead. 'I believe we can, Sarah. It may not be conventional, but it'll be real. I've learned that family isn't always about blood; it's about taking care of someone without counting the cost and without expecting anything.'

Sarah felt the weight of her father's words and knew they were rooted in years of love, mistakes, and lessons learned. 'I agree, Dad. And I promise to be there, holding your hand, holding Miguel's, and holding Ma's too.'

'Speaking of promises,' Jorge added, looking thoughtful, 'I've been contemplating what you said earlier about your mother and me dating other people. You may be right. But for now, I'm focusing on fixing our strained family ties. Happiness will come when the time is right.'

Sarah grinned, comforted by this affirmation. 'That's a good perspective, Dad, but, you have to think about yourself too. Both of you deserve happiness.'

The sun began to dip below the horizon, casting a golden glow that seemed to encapsulate the beauty and complexity of their relationship. Both father and daughter sat there, relishing the peace that had settled between them, excited for the new chapters that awaited their family.

'So,' Jorge started, 'how are you and Benito? Your mom filled me in on your new boyfriend. When am I going to meet him?'

Sarah took a deep breath, her eyes searching her father's, 'Our relationship is . . . it's going well. I love spending time with him. I'm rediscovering things about myself when I'm with him—my dreams, my aspirations, and the things I truly enjoy doing. I'll introduce you to him soon.'

'That's great, Sarah! I look forward to meeting Benito. And what about your job hunt?' Jorge asked.

'Dad, I got a good offer from another BPO.'

'That's great, Sarah. How did it go? Did you take it?'

'I surprised myself by turning it down. I'm not sure I want to go that track any more, especially after my waterfall trip and my blog.'

Jorge leaned back, taking a moment to collect his thoughts. 'Your BPO job was stable. Were you happy there?'

'Yes, it was stable. I was happy enough. But, I was much happier after meeting Marley and going on the waterfall trip.'

'Maybe you just needed a break. Are you sure you want to give up your BPO career?'

'For me, it wasn't just a break. I got to know myself more. I don't want to go back to a nine-to-five.'

'Then it's good you discovered that. As for what you want to do professionally, follow your passion, not just a pay cheque. Don't let the job define you; you define the job.'

Sarah smiled. 'I'll keep that in mind. Actually, I've been thinking of taking my blog to the next level, maybe even making it a full-time gig. I've gotten thousands of followers since I started. And I've monetized a bit with ads. I could still do more. I want it to be a full-time business now.'

Jorge smiled, 'That sounds like a fantastic idea. You have a gift for storytelling, Sarah. Don't let it go to waste. And starting your own business. Wow. You're much braver than me, Sarah.'

Sarah felt her heart swell. 'Thanks, Dad. That means a lot to me, especially coming from you. What about you, Dad? Are you still happy in your job? Did you ever think of doing something else?'

'My job has been my constant. I was good at it, and I'm *still* good at it. But you know what, now that I'm much older, I realize that my job won't love me like my family would. That's the thing with a job. You give it just enough so you can have a life too.'

They spent another hour talking—about Sarah's new relationship with Benito, about Jorge's retirement plans, and even about setting up a family outing soon, with Miguel and Helen included.

Finally, it was time to leave. As they stood up to go, Jorge hugged Sarah tightly, as if trying to make up for all the lost years in one embrace.

'I love you, Sarah,' he whispered, his voice tinged with emotion.

'I love you too, Dad,' Sarah replied, her eyes glistening with tears of relief and new-found happiness. 'I'll give you a call, okay? I need to ask you stuff about my business.'

'Call me anytime, Sarah. I'm not going anywhere.'

CHAPTER 32

Sarah and Marley sat at a cozy table tucked in the corner of their favourite café. The air was redolent with the aroma of freshly ground coffee beans and baked pastries. With laptops open and an eclectic mix of documents strewn across the table, it was evident they were on the cusp of something significant. Each had an iced latte in hand, and the mood was a fusion of casual camaraderie and serious business brainstorming.

'Thanks for helping me with this business, Marley. You're the more successful blogger between us two. I know you could have done this all on your own.'

'This idea was all yours, Sarah. If it weren't for you, I wouldn't be brave enough to start this on my own. Besides, us bloggers need to stick together.'

'I'm glad too!'

'So, where do we start?'

'Well, here's the grand plan,' Sarah began, her eyes sparkling with enthusiasm. 'We curate eco-tourism destinations, focusing initially on the Philippines. As locals, we have something that big travel agencies can't offer— an insider's perspective. We'll show people corners of the country that even Filipinos might not have explored.'

Marley looked intrigued as she took a sip of her coffee. 'I like where this is going, but we have to make sure it doesn't devolve into just another tour guide operation. What sets us apart?'

Sarah nodded knowingly, prepared for this very question. 'Three pillars—sustainability, education, and authentic experience. My trip to South Cotabato taught me that not every tourist destination has a happy story. The T'boli are struggling despite Lake Sebu being a tourist destination. We need to show people that every place they visit needs to be nurtured and protected too. Every destination we pick must practice sustainability, and this isn't negotiable. Second, we'll incorporate educational elements. Think nature conservation facts, historical trivia, and cultural immersion. Lastly, experience—tourists will taste local cuisines, perhaps partake in traditional storytelling sessions or even guided meditation in natural settings. What do you think?'

Marley's eyes widened. 'Sarah, this is brilliant. If executed well, it could be revolutionary. But how do we kick this off?'

'Digital presence,' Sarah answered. 'I'm in the process of upgrading my travel blog to a professional website. It's got decent traffic, and it can serve as a cornerstone for our online marketing initiatives. Think of it as a travel blog with an extended arm that actually lets people live those experiences.'

At this moment, Jorge Silvestre entered the café. Noticing his daughter deeply engrossed in discussion, he approached with a cautious smile. 'Mind if I join you? I couldn't help but overhear,' he said, gesturing towards an empty chair.

Sarah laughed. 'Oh, Dad, you know you're our main consultant today. Grab a seat,' Sarah invited, her heart grateful for her recent reconciliation with her father.

Jorge skimmed through some documents they had on the table. 'If you're serious about this, consider the power of branding. Develop a compelling brand story that combines your unique advantages—being locals with a first-hand perspective, for example. Use that story across all your social media platforms. Consistency is your friend here,' he emphasized.

Sarah took notes. 'This is great, Dad. Thank you.'

Jorge wasn't done. 'Don't forget revenue diversification. Your tours are just one aspect. What about merchandise? Local crafts, maybe, that you sell as souvenirs? Or even a subscription-based exclusive travel advice service? Partnerships are another avenue—local artisans, guesthouses, and eateries. Give them visibility on your platform, and they may offer your clients exclusive discounts. It's a win-win.'

Sarah and Marley exchanged excited glances. It was as if Jorge had illuminated a hidden pathway, one that promised adventure but also required meticulous planning and execution.

'Wow, Dad, that's a masterclass in Business 101,' Sarah chuckled, feeling a fresh appreciation for the man she had once been estranged from but was now so thrilled to have back in her life.

Jorge smiled, 'Well, when you've been in marketing and sales as long as I have, these things become second nature. But remember, the most important thing is to be passionate about what you're doing. The rest will follow.'

And so, the foundation was laid. Between Sarah's vision, Marley's operational skills, and Jorge's seasoned advice, it felt like the universe was finally aligning in Sarah's favour. It was the start of something new, something beautiful, and something incredibly significant. But above all, it was something that tied into Sarah's deeper sense of purpose— her love for travel and her insatiable curiosity about the world.

She felt it in her bones; this was *her* path, and she was ready to walk it, come what may.

'Dad, Marley and I want to ask you something,' Sarah said.

'Sure, what is it?' He looked at the two of them, smiling.

'We talked about it before we invited you over, and now we'd like to make it official. Can you join our team as a consultant?'

Jorge's eyes widened at first and then he broke into the biggest smile Sarah had ever seen on his face. 'I'm . . .' he hesitated, 'I'm so honoured.'

'We won't be able to pay you much at first—' Marley began.

'You could pay me one peso and I'd still like to keep this position, thank you,' Jorge joked.

'We'll pay you more than that, Dad,' Sarah replied. They all laughed.

'Welcome to the team, Dad,' Sarah said, giving him a heartfelt hug.

Two days later, Sarah found herself amidst a different yet equally enriching setting. She was in a quaint little restaurant with wooden tables and hanging plants, a perfect fusion of the rustic and the modern. Across from her sat Anya and Benito—her best friends, her anchors in her rapidly changing world. Today, however, the dynamics were slightly different. Benito was not just her best friend any more, he was her boyfriend, and the thought sent little flutters through her stomach.

'So, you're practically going to be a travel mogul now, huh?' Anya teased, taking a sip of her iced tea.

Sarah laughed, 'Oh, hardly. But I am venturing into new territories, and it's exciting.'

Benito looked up from his menu, his eyes meeting Sarah's. 'And I'm sure you'll excel, as you do in everything. But remember to take time for yourself too.'

Sarah felt a warm glow at his words. 'I will, I promise.'

The conversation flowed effortlessly, from Sarah's business plans to Anya's latest art project, and finally landing on Benito's recent bonus at work. Their little side trip to Davao had yielded a new business opportunity for Benito's family business and his dad had shared a generous cut of the profit with him. It was comfortable, it was familiar, but it was also tinged with a novel depth, a sense of possibilities and futures yet unexplored.

Anya leaned in, lowering her voice as if sharing a secret. 'Speaking of new territories, how's the love territory treating you two?'

Sarah and Benito exchanged glances, their eyes saying more than words ever could.

'We're taking it one adventure at a time,' Sarah finally answered.

Anya smiled, 'That's the best way to go about it. Life is too short for holding back on love.'

As they talked and laughed, Sarah found herself thinking about how much she had grown and how many aspects of her life had evolved. Her career, her friendships, and now her love life—they were all threads in her very own T'nalak dreamweave she was creating, day by day. It was far from complete, and that's what made it beautiful. The uncertainties, the challenges, the rewards—they were all part and parcel of this grand adventure called life.

Their food arrived, and as they began to eat, Sarah couldn't help but feel a sense of completeness. The restaurant was a cacophony of chatter and clinking plates, but in that moment, it was as if time had paused, allowing her to take stock of her blessings—her supportive friends, her loving boyfriend, her exciting new career, and the passion that fuelled her soul.

Benito, noticing her contemplative expression, asked 'What's on your mind?'

Sarah looked up, her eyes shimmering with unshed tears of happiness. 'Just thinking about how incredibly lucky I am to have you both in my life. You ground me.'

Anya reached across the table, placing her hand over theirs. 'And we're lucky to have you, Sarah.'

This was her tribe, Sarah realized—people who celebrated her victories, no matter how small; people who provided a soft landing during her falls, no matter how hard. In the grand scheme of her life's unfolding narrative, this moment was a quiet yet significant milestone, a reminder that while she may be 'Sarah, the Seeker' in her adventures, she was also 'Steadfast Sarah' in the intimate circles of her life.

Sarah was alone again that night, but she was far from lonely. Surrounded by the soft glow of her desk lamp, she opened her blog. From the private, sacred space of her journal, now Sarah felt she could write more easily for her community of followers on her blog.

The Seeker's Journey

Life has a funny way of surprising us. Just when we think we've figured out our path, it throws us a curveball—sometimes to challenge us, sometimes to bless us, and sometimes to do a bit of both. Just recently, I discovered that I want to be an adventurer, a traveller, a wanderer. But today, I realized something vital: I am also seeker.

There's a subtle difference, you see. An adventurer seeks thrills, a traveller seeks destinations, a wanderer seeks the unknown. But a seeker—well, a seeker looks for all of those things and more. A seeker looks for soul-deep experiences, for moments that change the essence of who they are.

Sarah paused, soaking in her own revelation. Her journey through the waterfalls had been transformational, yes, but the transformations had not just been external—they had penetrated the very core of her being.

And as I venture into this new chapter, alongside Marley, Anya, and Benito, I understand that the seeking never truly ends. There will be more waterfalls, more friendships, more love, and more self-discovery. But the best part? The seeking is not a solitary venture.

Because I've found my tribe—the people who seek alongside me, whether it's through the lens of eco-tourism, through the brushstrokes of a painting, or through the simple, profound act of loving another person.

She paused, as if hesitating to capture her next thought. But then, courage washed over her, and she continued.

*This new direction is both thrilling and daunting, but I am
guided by my passions. It's a risk, stepping into the unknown.
Yet, the most beautiful landscapes are often hidden behind the
thickest fogs, waiting to be discovered by those daring enough
to seek them.*

*So, here I am, standing at the edge of change, ready to
leap. My name is Sarah, and I am a Seeker. The destinations
are numerous, the paths are myriad, but the goal is singular—
seek, and you shall find.*

She closed her journal, her heart brimming with emotions
too profound for words. It was as if she had unlocked a new
level of self-awareness, one that empowered her to face the
challenges and opportunities that awaited her. She looked
around her room, her eyes lingering on her travel souvenirs,
her camera, and finally settling on a framed photograph of
her, Anya, and Benito.

As her eyes met her own reflection, Sarah knew, deep
down, that she was on the right track. The way ahead was not
without its uncertainties, and the terrain was unfamiliar. But
wasn't that the essence of every grand adventure?

Her mind was already racing with ideas for her next blog
post, her next travel destination, and her next business venture.
As she climbed into bed, she felt a sense of completeness
wash over her. It was a little scary, this new direction, but it
was a risk she was willing to take. After all, she was Sarah the
Seeker, and her journey was only just beginning.

And so, with a heart full of dreams and a soul eager to
explore, Sarah drifted off to sleep, ready for the adventures
that the new day would undoubtedly bring.

CHAPTER 33

'Guess what?' Sarah asked Benito as they hung out at her house.

'What?'

'Marley already registered our eco-tourism company with the Securities and Exchange Commission!' Sarah announced.

'When?'

'Just today.'

'What's next?'

'Local Government Unit registration and then we need to register with the Bureau of Internal Revenue.'

'That's wonderful. I've also been thinking.'

'About what?'

'About what we've seen together on our trip. It makes me rethink some things about real estate development.'

'That's big, Benito.'

'I know. It wouldn't have occurred to me if it weren't for your crazy waterfall adventure.'

'It wasn't *that* crazy.'

Since Sarah and Benito got back, Sarah had managed to beef up her travel blog, *Sarah, the Seeker*, with more 'Chasing Waterfalls' content. It was on the blog that Sarah made good on her word to Carmel that she would write about the T'boli and what they were facing.

Sarah had also already taken Benito along to Kinabuan Falls. Anya had complained that she was feeling a teeny bit left out, so they were already planning a trip with her to Batanes. 'Just don't nauseate me with all your couple stuff, okay?' Anya had asked them, 'Just stick to your room if you're going to go all gooey on each other. No PDA in front of me.' They'd had a good laugh over that.

'So, I heard about your dad from Tita Helen,' Benito said.

'Yeah, I saw him right on the day that we got back from Davao.'

'So, what happened?'

'Long story.'

'I don't mind long stories.'

'It was a cry fest.'

'Seriously?'

'He cried. Then I cried. It was like a telenovela in here.'

'I've always wondered about your dad.'

'Actually, me too.'

'So, what's going to happen?'

'He said he'd spend more time with me and Miguel.'

'Wow.'

'I know.'

'Are you going to introduce me?'

'Of course! I already promised him I would, but this whole business registration thing came along, and I got sidetracked.'

'How do you feel about the whole thing with your dad?'

'I thought I was going to be angrier. Strangely, I felt relief.'

'I'm not surprised. He's still a part of you, you know.'

'He got to answer questions that have been on my mind for a long time.'

'That's good.'

'And what about your fam? Do they know that we're . . . together?'

'They know. But it's still different if we make it official. Are you free next weekend?'

'What? That soon?'

'Hey, not soon enough. If you hadn't been so busy with your project with Marley, I would have wanted it earlier.'

'Well, it's the same for me, actually. Let's do it two weekends in a row. What do you think?'

'I think Steady Sarah is back.' They both laughed.

Sarah's phone started to ring. She looked down at the screen and saw that it was Pete. Sarah felt cold, her hands suddenly felt clammy. Instead of ending the call, she ended up passing on the phone to Benito who gave her a puzzled look.

'Hello?' She heard Benito say, 'Who's this?' And then after a heartbeat, 'Oh, Pete.' Benito took a look at her pale face and took the call outside.

Sarah waited in the sala. She thought she had been over Pete. She thought she was stronger than that. But apparently, one little phone call could still undo her after all.

'What did he want?' Sarah asked Benito as soon as he stepped in.

'He wants to meet you. You need to sign some paperwork for insurance.'

Oh, that. She'd forgotten about it.

'Sarah? Are you okay?'

'I'm just a bit shaken up. I'm sorry I handed you the phone. I should have faced up to him.'

'It's perfectly fine, Sarah. I totally understand.'

'I can't believe I caved in!' Sarah said, hating herself for not having the courage to talk to her ex.

'Sarah. Look at me,' Benito said, tilting her chin gently so that she could look straight into his eyes. Looking into his beautiful light-brown eyes calmed down the confused feelings that were imploding inside her.

'Sarah, I know you. You're going to spend the next hour obsessing over this.' Sarah didn't say anything. He was right.

'Sarah,' Benito continued, 'It's okay. You can relax. You don't have to pretend around me. You don't always have to be so strong. You can make mistakes. It's me. I will *never* leave your side.' Sarah couldn't help the tears that started to fall from her eyes.

'Did you tell him?' Sarah asked.

'About?'

'About us?'

'I think that's for you to tell him. I won't butt in when it comes to that,' Benito answered.

'Okay, you're right.'

'I love you, Sarah. Phone calls from exes and all.' He took her into his arms where she could do nothing but melt into him.

'I love you, Benito.'

She was dressed in a crisp white polo shirt, her favourite jeans, and black leather flats. She took a deep breath before entering the coffee shop where she and Pete had broken up. She didn't know why Pete chose to meet there. Habit maybe.

She still remembered how excited they had been when they had decided to get insurance together, assigning each other as beneficiaries. They were so sure about the state of their relationship then. 'When we get married, we can just update the paperwork,' Pete had suggested. They had gone out for a pizza and a beer at two in the afternoon. 'To us!' they had toasted.

And here she was, ready to end an investment that was supposed to have been part of their long-term plans.

Pete was already there. He looked a bit thinner but, otherwise, the same. She remembered the last time she saw him at the café. He'd looked harassed, with dark circles under his eyes. At least he looked more well-rested now.

'Hi, Pete,' she said. She tried her best to be civil.

'Hi, Sarah, you're looking well,' he said.

'Thanks.'

'Please, have a seat. I have the papers with me. It's pretty straightforward.' How formal they were, Sarah observed. She sat across him. He handed her a printout of the form. Most of the fields were already filled up. There was just a blank space for the new beneficiary. She and Benito had talked about it earlier. He told her that he didn't want her to feel any pressure at all. He said that assigning the insurance to her brother was fine in the meantime.

'Everything seems to be in order,' Sarah said.

'So, you're okay with the amounts?'

'Yes, Pete.'

'Good,' he said. He took out his own version of the insurance and showed it to her. It seemed that he had assigned a Joanna Cruz as the beneficiary. That stung a little. But that was his call. He was always going to do this. It was just a matter of which girl. In fact, the whole idea had been his after they had decided to open a joint account for the condo that they wanted to buy together. She wondered, briefly, if he had already set up another joint account with Joanna Cruz.

'This settles it. Thanks for trusting me to make all the arrangements,' Pete said.

He sounded like an efficient account manager.

'I can take care of having your papers notarized,' Pete said, 'Or do you want to take care of it yourself?'

'No, that's fine, Pete. You do it.'

'Okay. Once I've settled this with the insurance agent, I'll make sure to let you know. When it's turned over to you, you can upgrade the plan if you want. I'll send you all the details of the insurance agent so you can take care of making any future arrangements with him.'

'So, this is it?'

'That's it. It's all done. Well, almost all done.'

She realized that six years wasn't that easy to let go of. There was a time when she would have wanted the 'almost' part, just so she could see him again.

'Thanks for taking care of this, Pete.'

'It needed to be done, Sarah.'

'I went back to the condo, you know.'

'You did? The one in Pasig? Are you still planning to get it?'

'No. But it's funny. I said goodbye to it.'

Pete paused for a moment. 'That was a nice place.'

'It was.' The past tense had a bittersweet feel to it.

'Thanks for convincing me to get the insurance plan in the first place,' she said breaking the brief silence.

'The younger we get it, the better for us,' Pete replied.

Sarah smiled at the irony of it all. Insurance was supposed to be a protective buffer for all of life's uncertainties. So far, the past few months had been riddled with uncertainties. Would she tell him about Benito? Did he really need to know? They weren't together any more. She decided she didn't want to burn bridges.

'Uhm, Pete, I'm just letting you know, too, that Benito and I are together now.' She thought it was better this way. After all, after he'd have the insurance papers notarized, he'd need to call her again. She had saved Pete's number already. It was so immature of her to delete it in anger.

Pete smiled. 'Benito's a good guy.' It *was* a fact.

'Yes, that's right.'

'I'm happy for you, Sarah.' *Are you? Really?*

'You don't seem surprised. When we were together, did you ever think he liked me? I mean . . . as more than a friend?'

'He never outright said anything to me, Sarah. But I could see how devoted he was to you. That's why I'm not surprised.' Was it so obvious to everyone but her?

'I hope you're happy too, Pete.'

'I am. And since we're disclosing things—' Sarah had to smile at 'disclosing'. *What is this? A legal consultation?* '—I'm together with Joanna now.'

'Yes,' Sarah said, 'I noticed it in your paperwork.' *And not to mention your social media.* But Sarah was too embarrassed to bring that up.

The ink was still fresh on the paperwork they had just finished signing. It was done—their relationship was officially over. They looked at each other, not with sadness, but with a kind of mutual respect.

'You take care.' She didn't want to talk about Joanna further, but she hoped he got the point.

'You too, Sarah. I'll see you around,' he said.

'I'll see you around, Pete.'

There was an odd mix of feelings in the air. Relief, because they could now move on with their lives separately, without the strain of a relationship that no longer worked. Yet, there was also a hint of nostalgia, thinking back on the good times they had shared.

They said goodbye with a friendly hug, a clear sign they had moved on from being a couple to just acquaintances. Sarah appreciated this moment, this gesture. It was good to end things amicably.

Walking away, she felt a sense of finality. It was comforting to know they both wished the best for each other, even if a part of her couldn't completely let go of the past. This moment wasn't dramatic; it was simple, polite even, giving Sarah a little bit of peace.

Sarah walked out of the café with a light heart. She couldn't wait to meet up with Benito. *So, this is closure,* Sarah thought to herself. It wasn't all that bad.

CHAPTER 34

Sarah sat on the living room couch, flipping through an old family photo album. Helen was nearby, absorbed in a book. Sensing that this was the moment, Sarah closed the album and looked up.

'Ma, can we talk?' Sarah asked, her voice tinged with seriousness.

Helen put her book down and looked at her daughter, sensing the gravity in her tone. 'Of course, honey. What's on your mind?'

'It's about Miguel,' Sarah began cautiously. 'I think it's time he knows the truth about his biological dad.'

Helen visibly tensed. Her eyes narrowed, and for a moment, Sarah thought she saw a flash of fear. 'Why bring this up now? He's happy, Sarah. He's bonding with Jorge, and they're building a relationship.'

'That's exactly why we should tell him, Ma. He's getting close to Jorge, but what if he finds out the truth from someone else? Don't you think he deserves to know?'

Helen sighed, looking away as if the walls of the room could offer some guidance. 'He's just a kid, Sarah. I wanted to protect him from the complexities and pain that come with knowing he has another father out there somewhere.'

'Ma, Miguel is growing up,' Sarah countered, her voice tinged with urgency. 'And growing up means facing complexities and pain. I mean, if I were in his shoes, I'd want to know. Not just for the emotional aspect but also for practical reasons, like hereditary illnesses.'

Helen's eyes met Sarah's, a mixture of uncertainty and realization dawning in them. 'Do you think he's old enough, Sarah? He's only seventeen. Maybe we should wait a bit.'

'What are you so afraid of, Ma? You and Dad separated when I was seven. It was just a situation that was dumped on me. Did anyone think about whether I was old enough to deal with that?'

'That was different, Sarah.'

'I don't think this is too different. He's a teenager now, Ma. Don't you think it's better to tell him earlier rather than later? Do you want to shock him with this revelation when he's what, fifty?'

Helen shook her head, but she was in tears.

'Ma, I know you just want to protect him. But you can't protect him forever. He'll be in college soon. You owe this to him.'

Helen didn't speak, but she nodded.

Sarah felt a wave of relief wash over her. 'Thank you, Ma. It means a lot that you're willing to do this.'

Helen gave her a soft, sorrowful smile. 'It's time, isn't it? Okay, I'll talk to him.'

Sarah nodded. 'I'll give you two some privacy.'

As she picked up her jacket, Sarah couldn't shake off the weightiness of the moment. She knew that the upcoming conversation between her mom and Miguel would be a turning point in their lives, and the uncertainty of its outcome filled her with a mixture of hope and trepidation.

Sarah stepped into the coffee shop, its warm aroma immediately enveloping her. She ordered a cappuccino and took a seat near the window. The coffee shop was filled with the ambient noise of conversations and the clattering of cups and saucers, but all Sarah could focus on was the ticking of the clock on the wall.

As she sipped her coffee, her thoughts swirled in a mix of apprehension and second-guessing. *Did I do the right thing? Was I being fair to Ma, and more importantly, to Miguel?*

Her phone buzzed on the table, breaking her reverie. It was a text from Marley. The text was about a potential collaboration they had been discussing with a local resort.

She began to draft a response but stopped halfway. Her thoughts returned to her family, as they often did when she was away from them. She couldn't help but think of how much her own life had changed, and the lessons she'd learned along the way.

I've always believed in facing the truth, no matter how difficult, she thought. *And Miguel should have the chance to face his own truths. That's part of growing up, isn't it?*

She looked at the other patrons in the coffee shop, each absorbed in their world, each facing their own set of dilemmas and choices. *Life is a series of choices,* she mused. *We make decisions based on what we know, what we feel, and who we are. And those choices define us, for better or worse.*

It struck her that, by urging her mother to tell Miguel the truth, she was also offering him a choice. A choice to know his biological father, to grapple with complex emotions, and to decide what kind of relationship he wanted with the two most important men in his life.

The gravity of the situation began to ease a little. *No matter what happens, we'll face it as a family*, she thought, a strong conviction settling in. Sarah finished her coffee, left a tip, and headed for the door.

Time to go home.

Sarah turned the key in the lock and pushed the door open. The house was quiet, the air thick with the residue of a deeply emotional conversation. She found Helen and Miguel sitting on the living room couch, both looking a bit drained yet somehow lighter. Miguel's eyes met hers, and for a moment, a thousand words seemed to pass between them in silence.

'Hey,' Sarah said softly, taking off her jacket and joining them on the couch. 'How did it go?'

Miguel glanced at Helen before answering. 'It was a lot to take in, but I'm glad Ma told me. I'm still processing it all, but I'm okay.'

Sarah reached over and squeezed Miguel's hand. 'I'm here for you, no matter what you decide to do.'

Helen's eyes met Sarah's, a mixture of gratitude and relief visible in them. 'Miguel, your sister was the one who reminded me that you deserve to know the truth.'

Miguel nodded. 'And I appreciate that. It's something I needed to know. I'm just not sure what I'm going to do about it yet. For now, I don't think I'll be contacting my biological dad.'

Sarah nodded, respecting his decision. 'That's completely understandable. Take all the time you need.'

Helen cleared her throat, a hint of hesitation in her voice. 'Miguel, will this change how you see Jorge?'

Miguel took a deep breath before speaking. 'If anything, it makes me appreciate him more. To know that he accepted me as his son, no questions asked—that means everything to me.'

The room fell silent for a moment, each absorbing the weight and significance of Miguel's words. Finally, Helen spoke, her voice tinged with emotion.

'I love you both so much, and I promise that from here on out, we'll face everything as a family, no matter what comes our way.'

Sarah felt her eyes well up with tears as she looked at her mom and brother. This was a pivotal moment, a turning point, but it was also a reaffirmation of the bond they all shared. As they reached for each other, their arms forming a small but unbreakable circle, Sarah felt a sense of peace and assurance wash over her.

Life was a series of choices, and while they couldn't control the choices that were made for them, they could control how they reacted, how they loved, and how they supported one another. And for Sarah, that was all that mattered.

CHAPTER 35

Sarah sat at her mom's kitchen table, flipping through a travel magazine, when Helen walked in with an unusually radiant glow.

'You look happy, Ma,' Sarah observed, setting the magazine aside.

Helen beamed, 'Well, I had a wonderful night out.'

'A night out? With whom?' Sarah prodded, her eyebrows raised.

Helen hesitated for a moment, clearly debating how much to share. 'His name is Luis. We met at the community garden a few weeks ago, and well, we decided to go out for dinner.'

Sarah's eyes widened. 'Ma! You're dating? That's fantastic!'

Helen laughed, 'It's been so long, I'd forgotten how much fun it can be. Twenty-five years, Sarah! Can you imagine getting back into dating after twenty-five years?'

Sarah grinned. 'I can't, but I'm so happy for you, Ma. You deserve this.'

Helen walked over to her daughter and kissed her on the forehead. 'You reminded me that life doesn't stop, even when it feels like it has. I've got to keep living, keep experiencing new things. So, yes, I'm excited, and a bit nervous too.'

'Don't be nervous. You're a catch, and Luis is lucky to have the opportunity to get to know you,' Sarah reassured her.

Helen chuckled, 'Listen to you! Turning into the mom. But honestly, it feels like I'm out of practice.'

'Just get to know him better, Ma.'

'I'm too old for this,' Helen mock complained.

'No one's too old for love,' Sarah teased. She then grabbed her mom's hands. 'And I can't wait to hear all about it. Every single detail!'

Sarah walked into the rustic café where she was meeting Benito and Anya. She spotted them at a corner table, laughing. Anya was glowing, her face lit up in a way Sarah had not seen before.

'Hey, guys!' Sarah greeted, walking up to their table. They both rose to hug her, Anya more enthusiastically.

'Sarah! It's been too long!' Anya exclaimed.

'Way too long,' Sarah agreed, taking a seat. 'But look at you! Look at that tan!'

'I got inspired by your adventure, Sarah. I thought, *Why not take my own plunge?* So, here I am back from Siargao!'

'I'm so happy for you, Anya! I want to hear all about it.'

'That's awesome, Anya,' Benito chimed in, raising his glass. 'To taking plunges and finding happiness!' They all clinked their glasses together, sealing the moment.

As they enjoyed their drinks, the café door opened again, and in walked Marley, her face flushed, possibly from the sun or from the excitement of the day's work.

'Marley!' Sarah called out, waving her over.

Marley spotted the group. 'Hey, everyone!' she greeted, pulling up a chair next to Sarah, and broke into a smile. 'Business meeting ran late, sorry!'

'Business is good, I presume?' Sarah asked, her eyes twinkling.

'Fantastic,' Marley said, taking a sip of the iced tea that Benito ordered for her. 'Our eco-tourism venture is really picking up. Thanks to you, Sarah.'

Sarah waved her off. 'No, it's a team effort. You've been incredible.'

'Speaking of team effort,' Marley said, pulling out her phone. 'I just got an email from the Department of Tourism. They want to feature us in their next campaign!'

'That's huge!' Benito exclaimed.

Anya clapped her hands. 'Congratulations! I always knew you guys would make a mark.'

Sarah looked at Marley, their eyes meeting in mutual respect and excitement. 'See? I told you we were onto something big.'

Marley grinned. 'And to think this is just the beginning.'

CHAPTER 36

'Playlist?' Sarah asked Benito.

'Check!'

'Water and snacks?'

'Check!'

'Cell phone charger?'

'Check! Let's go already! We should be there by lunchtime!'

'Wait! I'm not done with the checklist on my app.'

'Sarah!'

'Okay, okay, let's go.'

Benito had just picked up Sarah from her house and they were on their way to Zambales.

Because of their new adventure lifestyle, Benito had got rid of his BMW and now drove a four-wheel drive with an eco-friendly diesel engine, instead. Sarah had also taken on bike-commuting from Marikina to Eastwood City where she and Marley sometimes met at their virtual office function rooms. They operated mostly from home and relied on the great website that Benito helped them design. Jorge had also taken care of some of their earlier lead-generation campaigns so they could do more on their own. They already had a few clients lined up from corporate social responsibility programmes to more enlightened tourists from Europe who didn't just want to enjoy themselves in the Philippines but really immerse themselves in the culture of the community they wanted to visit.

Apart from the eco-tourism company, Sarah also did consulting jobs for BPO training programmes. She realized that training was one aspect of her BPO job that she missed. So, after scouting around among her contacts, she found that training gigs were in demand, especially for people like her who had some experience in the field. That meant productivity at hours she could dictate. She'd never imagined that the life she had was possible. Well, that was also thanks in part to Marley who was a consultant as well, but for the NGO field. She'd shared with Sarah all her consultancy best practices, from looking for clients to creating billing statements for her consultancy hours. Marley was great at what she did. In no time, Sarah had been able to set up a separate BIR certificate of registration as a consultant.

'So, you're sure that we can just walk to the Pawikan Conservation Center from the beach we're staying at?'

'Yup! Hey, check the glove compartment, I got something for you.'

'Benito! What is it?'

'Just check it out.'

Sarah opened the glove compartment and saw two matching paracord bracelets with side-release buckles.

'Wow! Where'd you get these?'

'I made those.'

'No way, Benito! I didn't know you were into arts and crafts too.'

Benito laughed. 'Hey, these are manly arts and crafts.'

'Whatever! Wait! Did you put beads in them too? Benito, you've outdone yourself.'

'Count the beads.'

Sarah counted eight.

'Benito, these are the eight stones that chronicle my seven plus one waterfalls,' Sarah said softly.

'What about mountains next?'

'Why not?'

Sarah hit the shuffle play button on her phone and the first song was a song by Coldplay. Benito reached out for her hand and, even though it was as corny as ever, Sarah was glad to hold hands with him (and she was glad that the car was automatic too!). They had a whole wonderful weekend ahead of them. Sarah sang along. 'This one life. This one adventure.' She only wanted to share it with Benito.

ACKNOWLEDGEMENTS

Writing *Steady Sarah* has been an incredible journey, made possible by the support and contributions of many. I would like to express my sincere gratitude to:

Nora Nazerene Abu Bakar of Penguin Random House SEA, for choosing my novel pitch and making my dream of being a published author a reality.

Cassandra Chia, my structural editor, whose thoughtful and insightful recommendations greatly enhanced the depth and stakes of Sarah's journey.

Surina Jain, my copy editor, whose fact-checking and attention to detail ensured the accuracy and clarity of every page.

My husband, Vier, for his unwavering support and for providing valuable insights into Sarah's dilemmas.

My daughter, Clea, who, as one of my first readers (except for the adult parts haha), helped me see the narrative through new eyes.

The #RomanceClass community in the Philippines founded by Mina V. Esguerra, for creating an encouraging environment that got me started writing romance.

My sister, Mercedes, for sharing her experiences in the business process outsourcing industry, which added authenticity to parts of the story.

My father, Augusto, for regaling us with tales of Mindanao from his business trips and introducing durian to us kids.

Aurora M. Suarez, Mina V. Esguerra (again), and Samantha Sotto Yambao, for generously facilitating the Write Away Retreat in 2017, inspiring me to continue writing novels and to bravely pitch to publishers and agents.

My family and friends, whose belief in me and constant encouragement have been a source of strength and motivation.

Finally, a nod to the natural wonders of the Philippines—the waterfalls, rivers, beaches, lakes, mountains, and underwater marvels that not only serve as settings in the novel but also inspire its spirit.

Thank you all for being part of this adventure.